Bad CONNECTIONS

HORROR STORIES

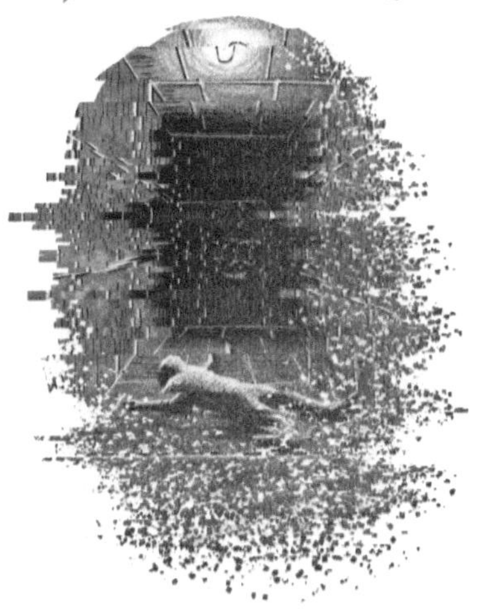

by Ryan C. Bradley

Illustrated by Eva Mout

"No Point Crying" originally appeared in *Dark Moon Digest* #42.
"Safe at Home" originally appeared in *Sorry, We're Closed.*
"Jailbreak" originally appeared in *Tales to Terrify* #616.
"Catholic Guilt" originally appeared in *Gothic Blue Book V: The Cursed Edition.*

ISBN: 979-8-218-47798-1

First Edition

RyanCBradley.com

Contents

No Point Crying

IT WAS AFTER FIVE and Mariano was alone in his cubicle, clacking away at the keyboard. He was almost grateful when Kevin Pilmento, whom he hadn't talked to in years, texted him, "Everything good, bro?" with a picture of a milk carton. The black letters at the top read: MISSING. Underneath was a photo of Mariano. Blonde hair, dark blue eyes, mid-level cheekbones, and a smidge of fat under the chin. In the picture, he was wearing the same blue shirt and the red tie he wore for the first time today.

Mariano popped his head out of the cubicle like a prairie dog and looked around for who might've taken the picture. He was in a sea of barren desks. The mortgage due notices and checks they processed were confidential, so being messy wasn't an option. It was the neatest office Mariano had ever worked in, which suited him. He hated being the cleanest person.

"B for execution, D- for a dumb idea," Mariano texted back. "How did you get my picture?" Did those pictures even show up on milk cartons like that anymore? Who was responsible for putting them on there? What adult drank out of milk cartons?

"No joke. Hope everything is well," Kevin texted back almost immediately. This time he'd attached a zoomed-out photo with his face next to the milk carton.

Mariano emailed both pictures to himself so he could see them on his bigger computer screen. He zoomed in and looked for the telltale bulges of a doctored image. He couldn't find anything, but that didn't mean it wasn't photoshopped. It meant Kevin was better at manipulating images than Mariano was at detecting them.

Mariano wasn't missing, anyway. He was where he should be, at his job, struggling to climb the corporate ladder. Where or how Kevin still had the time for this kind of bullshit was a question Mariano couldn't answer.

WHEN MARIANO GOT HOME, he tried to have a regular night. He got takeout from the restaurant below his apartment—tonight was orange chicken—and ate on the sofa. He didn't watch the TV, but he left it on for the illusion of company.

His phone rang. He'd scaled his mother's calls from once a day to once a week. He let the first one go through to voice-mail. They talked on Sundays, on weekends when neither of them was traveling or had other plans. It was Wednesday. When she called again, instead of letting her leave a message, he picked up.

"Hello," he said, feigning sleepiness though it was only 9:30.

"I was hoping to catch you awake," she said. She sounded, as always, enthusiastic. She put energy into everything she said. He might've found it endearing in someone else's mother.

"I'm awake now."

"I saw something strange today."

He pictured her, the wire of the corded phone she refused to replace wrapped around her index finger, squeezing the tip red.

"What's that?" Mariano said.

"At school, there was a milk carton with your face on it that said 'Missing.'"

There was a long pause.

"Did Kevin put you up to this?" he said.

"Kevin who?"

"Kevin Pilmento." He sighed.

"You don't know anything about it?" She'd be chewing her lip now.

On the TV, a man in a surgical gown was weighing a heart on a scale next to an autopsied corpse. "No, Mom. I'll call them tomorrow."

"I could call."

"No, Mom. Don't worry, I'll do it."

"Will you let me know what you find out?"

The problem with phone conversations with his mother was that they never ended. "Of course. I better get to sleep, though."

She sighed. "Love you."

He hung up.

HE SLIPPED FROM the 13th-floor lunchroom to the quiet reading room down the hall after he finished eating the next day. It had two shelves filled with the toss-away books his coworkers were too lazy to bring to the library. He closed the door to block out the sound of the infuriating game of Uno his coworkers played during lunch.

After two rings, a computer answered. He skipped the menu by saying that he had information about one of the missing, which was technically true. More accurate would be that he had information on someone who wasn't missing.

The woman who answered the phone had a warm voice, though he couldn't tell if it was from an outgoing personality or her being good at her job.

"I'm calling in regard to the missing person on carton #35453. Mariano Baker," he said.

She typed something into her computer. "Do you have any information about Mr. Baker's whereabouts?"

"This is him."

"Baker is a very common name," she said. "As is Mariano."

"It's my picture, too. How many Marianos are Bakers, and how many Marianos have blue eyes and blonde hair?" His half-Mexican, half-Czech mother had named him after two Uncle Marianos she'd had in Mexico. The first became a priest, so they'd named the second Mariano, too.

"Sir, there is a serious fine for tying up official lines." The warmth from her voice had gone.

"It's my name and picture on that carton, and I'm not missing."

"I am tracing the call. If you do not have information about missing person #35453, I seriously suggest you hang up this phone right now."

"I'm right here. Take my photo off the carton and put on someone who needs it." He hung up, wishing that cell phones could give the satisfaction of slamming down a landline.

THURSDAYS, MARIANO SMUGGLED his bat bag into work and hid it under his desk. At five he promptly left for the batting cages across the street and hit for an hour. He had two bats—a Derek Jeter and a Joe Mauer. He loved Derek Jeter the ballplayer, and he'd hit a few with it every time he went to the cage, but the Joe Mauer was his ideal bat. The handle was a perfect fit and the head a good weight for turning on a ball.

The cages had a protective fence around the back, but Mariano cracked a few with the Mauer that would've gone out of a real park. He missed the game. He'd played through high school and he was almost good enough for college, but not quite. He wanted to play more while he still had his stroke, but he didn't have time for a beer league.

He squared his feet and brought the bat up.

Mariano wished he was facing a pitcher instead of a machine. The thrill of baseball was that duel. The stare down. The leg kick. Both men trying to outsmart. To overpower. To out speed. He relished losing for the moments when he connected. What Mariano needed in his life was to stop hitting rubber balls shot out of a machine and get back into the real world of competition. He needed the thrill of knowing he'd won, even if he'd lost the last four.

He rocked back on his feet and then forward to crush another ball.

HE WENT BACK to Szechuan Wok and ordered dumplings and rice and waited in the restaurant. The man behind the counter recognized him and threw in a few extra fortune cookies.

Mariano lugged his bat bag and dinner up the three flights of stairs. He paused at the alcove when he saw the package in front of his door. Neither the mailman nor the special delivery guys brought things past the entryway because there wasn't an elevator. Even if they had, he hadn't ordered anything. He approached it slowly, as though it were a bomb. For all he knew, it was.

He dropped his dinner and his bag six feet from the box. It was nondescript cardboard. It gave him the same feeling from when he was a kid and he'd seen lightning strike the neighbor's house. No one had believed him, but a few seconds before it hit, he'd known something terrible would happen. It was like something jangling his spine.

He unzipped his bag. He held the Joe Mauer like a samurai rather than a ballplayer. He tapped the top of the package from a distance. Nothing happened. He tapped again, and when he was sure that it wouldn't explode, he came closer. Unless it was on the bottom, there was no address or sender anywhere on the box. He pushed it with his foot. It was too heavy to budge. He tried to nose one of the flaps open with the bat, but it was taped shut. He used his keys to tear the tape.

Inside were full red-and-white, school-lunch milk cartons, stacked in alternating layers of upside down and right-side up. Each had a picture of Mariano's face under the word MISSING.

———

HE'D GOTTEN THE takeout containers open, but he'd only managed to eat half a dumpling. His fork stood upright in the other half, and then tipped over, falling like a tree. He'd taken out his pen and clicked it to the rhythm of "Umbrella," or as close to it as he could get with the pen's reset time. He wasn't fond of the song, but the music that slipped into and out of his head through the day had a will of its own.

Kevin seemed like a dead end. He wouldn't have the resources to pull this off as a prank. Whoever sent this package delivered it personally or sent it by courier service. But who? Why?

He walked out into the hallway. There were no clues, so he didn't know what he expected to find. He didn't have a blacklight or anything comparable. Mrs. Goldfarb rarely left, so he knocked on her door across the hall.

Mariano would peg her at about 80 years old. He secretly feared becoming the neighbor in the news story that investigates a rotting smell across the hall and finds a body. She opened the door in her nightgown and sleeping cap.

"I'm sorry to bother you," he said. "I'm Mariano Baker from across the hall."

"I know. The one with no friends," she said.

He ignored the jab. "I got a package earlier and I was wondering if you saw who dropped it off?"

Her eyes narrowed. This had been a bad idea. "I saw an unmarked box sitting there. What was in it?"

"Milk," he said. Maybe he should've lied, but this whole

thing felt so strange he wondered if he could identify reality well enough to know if he was telling the truth or not.

"They haven't delivered milk to people's doors in years. Is this some kind of internet thing?"

"No." He considered. "It could be. I don't know."

She squinted at him. "Are you on drugs?"

"Nothing was written on the box. I was hoping you'd seen something. They've got my picture on them."

Mrs. Goldfarb nodded slowly. "Did you put the milk in the fridge?"

"Excuse me?" he said.

"Did you put the milk in the fridge? I don't care what you do across the hall, but if that stench floats across to my apartment, you're invading my space."

How long had it been out? It could be spoiled already. It was a hot summer. "I'm going to do that now," he said.

"You want some advice?"

He paused at his door. "Sure."

"Buy some cereal." She closed her door. The chain clinked on the other side, leaving Mariano alone again with his cartons.

The 48 cartons took up most of his fridge. It had been empty except for leftover soy sauce, half a dozen eggs, a quarter of a lime, and two bottles of sriracha. He made a point of facing each carton so the cartoon cow looked out. At least the picture was still from the day before. He hadn't been photographed a second time. Being an adult meant that he needed to stop striving for things to get better and start settling for them not getting worse.

———

A HALF HOUR before lunch the next day, Sonia called him into her office. She was impressively stern. That's why the two of them got along. They didn't play Uno at lunch or go to the "secret" office happy hour every Thursday. They were the kind of people who understood that work was work. They were at Baltimore Private to climb as high as they could.

"Did something happen last night?" Sonia said after she'd shut her door. Her name was on a golden plaque in the center of her immaculately clean desk.

There were no pretenses. No small talk. Mariano liked that. He was tempted to tell her about the milk, but he wanted the promotion more than he wanted to figure out what the hell was going on. "Nothing spectacular. My air conditioner stopped working in the night and it was hard to sleep in the heat."

"Varun's got no problem sleeping," she said. "He's got no problem getting a promotion, either."

Varun. He worked two cubicles down from Mariano. He was tall and gangly, like a boy who'd just hit puberty. Mariano couldn't recall hearing him speak. Of course, Sonia loved him.

"I'm sorry," Mariano said. "I called maintenance, and they're going to fix my unit. This won't happen again."

AT LUNCH, Mariano ate his leftover dumplings. His appetite had come back in a big way. The Uno game at the center table still irked him. Playing cards was fun but he hated table talk. He'd played Uno at summer camp. At most games, he was a cut above the other kids. Something about the way his mind functioned had him winning more games than not, certainly doing better than random chance. He did it quietly, not feeling the need to brag, but once he'd won a few, the ganging up would start. A table of kids keeping track of what colors he'd played and which ones he didn't and shouting it out. They would reverse away from him and set each other up to give him plus two chains that left him with half the deck in his hands. With kids it had been bad. With these adults, hearing the table talk of a game he wasn't playing in was unbearable. The worst part was that they weren't even good at it.

"He's got a red. Nobody play a red," a blonde woman, whose name he'd forgotten, said.

"I can reverse away from him," said Albi with his Lithuanian accent.

If they really wanted to win, they should've been worried about getting their own cards down. Fixating on the competition obscured their own path to victory. He couldn't stand it.

Mariano scarfed down the last of his dumplings and slipped out of the lunchroom.

MARIANO GOT A six pack of beer on his way home. It was Friday and he was going to enjoy himself. Three tonight and three Saturday. That would get him buzzed enough to sleep better. When he opened the fridge to put the beer away, all 48 milk cartons had been turned so his face was looking outward. He hopped back with a little scream and dropped the beer. Two bottles broke. Foam flooded his kitchen. Shards of glass floated down the brown river.

"Shit," Mariano said. He'd grabbed a roll of paper towels to stop the flow before it got to the carpet when he heard footsteps in his apartment.

He threw the towels down near the middle of the stream. He grabbed a carving knife. His front door opened into a hallway that he had to cross to get into the kitchen. His bedroom shared a wall with the kitchen, and the hallway ended in his living room. He wouldn't be frightened out of his own home.

He kicked off his shoes and crept down the carpeted hallway. He held the knife out in front of him. The bedroom door he'd left open was closed. He took a second to pull himself together.

He twisted the knob. This might've started as a prank, but breaking into his apartment was too far. He opened the door.

His bed with its purple sheets was made. The closet was ajar, but empty. The TV was off. Everything was in perfect order. His gym stuff was under the bed, so there'd be no room for a person there. He pointed the knife behind him in case whatever he'd heard tried to sneak up on him. He sat down on the bed. Was it possible that he'd had some kind of dissociative break and he'd somehow done all of this to himself?

He stepped back out into the hallway and closed the door. If someone was there, they'd need to make a noise to enter the bedroom. The living room opened off away from the hallway. He reached the corner and pressed against the wall. The plan was to pivot and stab. He knew where the furniture was, so if no one was there, he wouldn't hit anything. If someone had broken in and was waiting for him in that blind spot, he'd kill them. His fear stopped him from thinking through the ramifications. He stepped and stabbed, but the living room was empty, too.

He fell onto the leather couch and dropped his knife on the coffee table.

"Shit," he said. The beer would be soaking into the carpet by now.

When he'd finished sopping up the beer and sweeping the broken glass, Mariano called the super. He knew that he'd be lucky to catch the actual super, but his building was run by a large enough management group that they'd have guys on call. Not that they'd ever been helpful in the past, regardless of how much Mariano paid.

"Samberg Emergency Line. Glenda speaking. How may I help you?"

"Hi. I live in apartment 12a of the Roosevelt Building. I'd like to have my lock changed."

"And why is that, Sir?" Glenda asked him. The world was full of lazy people who didn't want to do their jobs. He hated them all. Glenda especially.

"Someone broke into my apartment while I was at work today."

"Was anything taken?"

"No. It was out of order, though."

"Then how are you sure someone broke in? Could you've forgotten where you put those things?"

"Not a possibility."

"Why not?"

He slipped his pen out of his pocket and clicked it repeatedly. "Because it was a lot of stuff."

"What exactly was moved?"

"The milk in my fridge." He realized how ridiculous it sounded and tried to correct course. "This wasn't just one container. This was 48 cartons." He clicked the pen faster.

"You want me to send the locksmith because someone broke into your apartment and moved 48 milk cartons?"

"I know this sounds crazy, but I can pay for the locksmith. I'll pay for your time, too."

He waited to hear a click or Glenda's voice.

"You sound frightened," she said.

"Someone came into my house while I was at work." He put the pen down.

"I'm sorry, but the locksmith is out until Monday. Do you have a friend you can stay with until then?"

"No," Mariano said. "There's no way he could come any earlier?"

"It's not feasible."

He opened his wallet and counted the money. "I've got 90 bucks, in cash. He comes tonight and he can have it."

"We aren't allowed to take tips."

"Could you relay that message at least?"

"He'll come by on Monday. You'll just have to wait until then. I can get you the number for a local hotel."

"Will Samberg put me up?"

"Unfortunately, that wouldn't be a possibility."

"Thanks. Have a safe night." He dropped his head down onto his kitchen table.

———

HIS APARTMENT HAD six windows. Two on the back wall of each room. He had central air that regardless of what he'd told Sonia, kept his apartment cool all summer. He stuck a piece of clear plastic tape on each. The strip would rip if the windows were opened. At least he'd know how the intruder got in. He set the Derek Jeter under the bottom of the front door. The bat wasn't big enough to jam it shut, but the door swung inward. The bat would clatter if someone opened it.

He tucked the Joe Mauer under the sheets with him. If someone came, he'd clobber them. The thought was reassuring, but it didn't help him as he tried to drift off into sleep.

IN THE NIGHT, Mariano woke over the toilet, vomiting milk.

THE SUN STARTED its slow ascent a bit before six but hadn't risen enough to light his room. He felt groggy, but he grabbed the bat he'd slept with and sat up. There was a milk carton on his nightstand. The mouth was open and facing him. He pressed back against the backboard and flicked on the lamp. The shadows in the corners of the room disappeared. No one was immediately visible. He stretched toward the bottom of the bed slowly, ready to swing, though he wouldn't be able to put much force behind it as he lay prone. He lifted the dust cover. There were only the dust bunnies he should've cleaned weeks ago. His closet was open. There wasn't space for a person to hide in there without throwing out some shoes. He jabbed the barrel of the bat through anyway. He noticed a second carton on the floor among the shoes.

He couldn't tell much from it. Whoever had put it there drank all of it but the dredges on the bottom. Then he noticed the new text underneath his picture:

"Missing Since 8-13-16."

Today.

MARIANO DIDN'T GET UP for breakfast or leave the bed other than to check the door. It had been locked when he went to bed, but now it was unlocked. He sat with his bat in one hand and phone in the other. The bat drooped, resting on the covers. When seven came around, he called his mother.

"Mariano, hi! I wasn't expecting to hear from you today. Is everything okay?"

He rubbed the beginnings of a beard that had cropped up overnight. "Not good, Mom."

"What's wrong?" Something about her voice transported him back to being six years old with a scraped knee and a dinged-up bike.

"The milk carton."

It took her a moment to register what he was saying. "You mean the one with your picture on it? Did you ever call them?"

He broke down and the whole thing poured out. The call to the people who made these things. The package. Mrs. Goldfarb. The super. The carton by his bed with that day's date on it. He rambled achronally, throwing in details from different parts of the stories as they came to him. Finally, he told her what he'd been needing to tell someone since he'd moved to Baltimore: "I'm so goddamned lonely."

"I think you need to come back to New York," she said. "Being away is hurting you."

"It's not being alone. It's being watched that's driving me crazy. Someone put a milk carton on my nightstand. They're crazy, not me."

"Honey, just for the weekend. If you left now you could be here by lunch. I want to see how you're doing in person."

"What if we Skyped?" He didn't want to drive to New York. The traffic on Saturdays was brutal. This was why he limited their conversations. The more she got of him, the more she wanted, like an addict.

"It's not the same," she said.

"Do you want to smell me or something?"

"I'm worried about you. Do you hear yourself? Who's after you? The milkman?"

"Listen, I've got to go, Mom. I need to do laundry."

"Don't shut me out when you need me."

"Love you," he said, hoping to hear it back but unwilling to wait.

"Maybe I can drive down," she said.

He hung up. He threw the phone on the bed and lay back. He hadn't slept much and knew he wouldn't that day. Not with the impending threat of whatever was going to take him looming.

He wouldn't be roused for food, but he got out of bed for coffee. Delirious, he said, "And I can put as much milk in it as I want." He laughed, at first staccato syllables, and then doubled over.

When he'd gotten the giggles out, he opened the door. Six cartons were positioned around it, as though they were waiting for him.

"Holy shit," he shouted and swung the bat and hit one. It was strange and leathery, not like paper. They'd felt normal when he'd loaded them into the fridge. He listened for a creak, a step, breathing, anything to tip him off to the presence of someone else in the house. He could see the front door. The Derek Jeter hadn't been moved.

The windows. He had to check the tape. He went back into the bedroom first. The tape was untouched. Milk cartons lined the windowsill in the living room. He brushed them off with the bat. That tape was intact, too. He headed for the kitchen. There were more cartons on the table and the counter. They were all open with only an almost-translucent layer of liquid left on the bottom. He ignored them and went straight for the windows. That tape hadn't been broken either.

No one had been inside the apartment. Or they'd been here all along. Or he'd done this himself.

He turned on the coffee maker. If he couldn't have answers, he'd have caffeine. He heard cardboard scraping on the floor behind him and spun around. The cartons had gotten closer. They were surrounding him.

"What the fuck," he said. He squished another one. It resisted when wet cardboard should've crumbled.

The fridge door swung open. The first carton fell out as though it had leaped. The rest that followed erased all doubt.

They were piling out on their own. The cartons had emptied themselves in the night and they were coming for him.

"Shit, shit, shit," he said. He raised the bat over his head and brought it down onto one. It crumpled around the barrel. It reformed when he lifted the bat. His back pressed against the counter. He kicked one away, but the other 47 advanced. He climbed onto the counter and opened the window behind it. It was a three-story drop, but he could land in the dumpster. He fumbled with the releases of the screen. The cartons crept closer. When his thumb slipped a second time he thrust the bat through the screen. He kicked the closest carton away from him. He swept the bat over the counter and knocked more off. He went to jump.

A green light shot out of a carton and onto his calf. It shone from his knee to the ball of his foot. There was a slurping sound and the area that the light touched looked as though it were in a blender. It was painless after the initial clamp. Mariano didn't know if it was shock or some kind of anesthetic mercy. He didn't care. He could live without a foot.

He used his arms to push halfway out. The cartons bit in three places at once. His neck, his left elbow, and his right shoulder all turned green.

Mariano made it halfway through the window and found himself looking into the eyes of an old man in a window in the building across the alley. The old man yanked his curtains shut. In that moment of hesitation, the cartons dragged Mariano back into the apartment.

———————

IN NEW YORK, his mother would call the police, who wouldn't act until they got another call from Sonia when Mariano no-showed, no-called at work on Monday. His mother would regret not driving down after the call on Saturday, but he'd told her not to.

She liked to imagine him alive somewhere, happy on a beach, finally relaxing. She could almost find the strength to forgive herself when she thought about him this way.

IN A FACTORY, an unmarked package slides down a conveyor belt. It stops in front of a man with a hard hat who opens it. He counts off 48 full milk cartons and makes a note on his clipboard. He tapes the box shut and sends it to its next stop.

Safe at Home

THERE'S NOTHING QUITE as good as being young and in love. Except maybe drugs. Although, drugs can have lasting side effects, whereas love's only potential downfall is pregnancy. Be honest, would you rather crack a knuckle and go on an unexpected acid trip or spend nine months with a parasite growing to the size of a pumpkin inside of you? I know my answer and, more importantly, Reynolds knows my answer.

No, not Burt Reynolds, though I sometimes see the resemblance, too. My boyfriend Paul is also last-named Reynolds. I refuse to call him Paul, though. Pauls are serious men that work on computers and have no souls. Reynolds is the kind of man who would climb a tree to save a cat that had gotten itself stuck. A Paul wouldn't. Thus, Reynolds. He's got spiky cool-guy hair and he's strong enough to carry me down five flights of stairs, though he has to put me down at the landings on the way back up. It gets all of his blood rushing and his arms look huge afterward, but we can't really bone because of the cast. Don't get me wrong, we do other things that are nice, but some actual penetration would be wonderful.

He was doing all this carrying because I'd pulled a Kennedy drinking and skiing. What can I say? Massachusetts born and raised. I took a jump, didn't get my tip up high enough for the landing, and crack. There went my fibula. In most ways, though, I was lucky. How many skiers die per year? Fifty-four out of every million do in the U.S. When your leg is broken and you live on the fifth-floor walkup, no question is too unimportant for thorough research, or, in this case, googling how many skiers die per year. There's time to exhaust the content on your high school boyfriend's Netflix account. Time to write 50 pages of *Hunger Games* fan fiction and read it to your poor boyfriend when he gets home from work. Time to peep on the legged through the window.

Today, I watched a fence be assembled. It came in spools so big it took two beefy construction workers to get them upright. Their arms quivered under their sweaty, clinging neon-green t-shirts as they unfurled the rolls of linked metal. They'd poured concrete around the poles earlier this week, and a third worker followed them, fastening the chain link with a tool I couldn't see. They were fencing in an elevated asphalt patch under a defunct overpass across the street from my building. The new fence cut us off from the subway entrance, so we'd have to circle the station to get to work. Wonderful. A detour for when I got my walking boot next week. Nothing heals a broken leg like walking an extra block and a half.

The newly fenced Roland Overpass was built in 1951 so cars would be able to pass through our neighborhood without having to stop. It was named in honor of Monsignor Casey Roland, an Irish bishop who fought for the rights of the people of our neighborhood against big lobbies. He lost, obviously, if they put up an overpass to divert traffic away from local businesses, but he'd tried. Around these parts that's enough to get the thing you tried to prevent named after you.

There is a stark divide between people who want it torn down and people who want it to stay up. Those in favor of destruction do not live in the neighborhood but hold elected positions and believe tearing down ol' Roland will mean more walking and cycling and less motor-vehicling. Those opposed live in the neighborhood and understand what a shit show it will be. Personally, I believe in taking it down so I can see further from my window, which as I mentioned, is my main form of diversion after Netflix and my *Hunger Games* fanfic.

People too cool or unaverse to risks will hop the fence once they've crossed New Jefferson Street. Reynolds will not. He loves rules, even though losing time bothers him.

He's still not home. Nine more days until I'm in a walking boot and back to work.

2/21/15 (EARLY EVENING)

I hope no one thinks I'm a dweeb (although if you're reading my journal and judging me harshly, stop reading it, asshole) but I geeked out a little too hard when I saw Reynolds coming from the train station. I had my cast in the windowsill, along with my glass of water. I hopped when I saw him, and I spilled the water onto the bed and all over myself. The good news is Reynolds is muy guapo, and he'll be upstairs soon to dry me. The bad news is we keep the window cracked in the winter because our furnace's only settings were off or boiling and we needed to even it out. The wind breezing in might literally freeze to me. I hope I can think of something cool to say when he gets here. Maybe I'll say seeing him made me wet.

2/22/15 (EARLY MORNING)

I woke up in the night, pain surging, incredibly thirsty. The Vicodin (prescribed, not illegal, though I am not the littlest bit opposed) had worn off as I slept. I could feel the geology of my bones resetting. I sat up and through the window saw a figure in the center of the fenced-in area. A shadow that no one or nothing was casting. I knew it was two in the morning without looking at a clock—heavy painkillers teach you to know exactly when you need another dose—and that the station had been closed for an hour.

It could've been anywhere from six to eight feet tall. From five stories up, I'd have needed something to scale it against to say for sure. Where its face should be, the darkness thickened.

It turned toward me, and I could feel it watching me, like it was behind me and in front of me all at once. My stomach soured. I smelled something like rotten eggs and fell on my back, eyes on the ceiling. I collapsed onto the bed.

The wind seeped through the cracked window. The smell began to dissipate, and I shook Reynolds. He mumbled something incoherent. I waited a second, trying to reassemble my consciousness. Maybe I had hallucinated it. I'd been seeing bugs. I shook Reynolds again. The sweat puddled in the bottom of my cast. The pain rode the waves of my quickening pulse. I checked if it was still there.

It must've been waiting for me. Four more shadows blossomed out of it, all connected to the original branching out in the cardinal directions. I wanted to hurl. All five heads turned toward my window and I fell back again. It knew I was here. The question was, did it care?

I made sure that I woke Reynolds this time. "I don't wanna," mumble, mumble. I did it again harder.

"Get up."

"What?" His voice heavy with sleep. He looked around the room before noticing me lying next to him.

"Why'd you wake me?" he asked, words peanut buttered with sleep.

"Look out the window," I said.

He leaned over me. I wasn't sure if he saw it or not until he jerked back like he'd been burned. "What the fuck?"

"When I saw it, it saw me," I said.

"Why is it looking at us?" he said. The rotten-egg smell wafted back into the room. I pinched my nose.

"I don't know," I said. "You see it though, right?"

The ceiling fan above us cast a shadow onto the bed. "Yes," he said. He waved his hand in front of his face, ineffectually fanning at the smell.

"Do you have your phone?" I said. I knew he didn't. He insisted we charge them across the room, where the signals wouldn't give us cancer, or would at least give us cancer more slowly. I couldn't exactly get mine, though.

"Who am I going to call?" he said.

"The police," I said.

"And say what?"

He had a point there. There wasn't really much we could say. And then, I said, "Tell them that someone is trespassing in the station. They'll come by to check it out."

We argued, then he called.

We stayed prone while we waited, fingers interlocked. We didn't talk. We didn't whisper. We didn't sleep. We were as still as I can ever remember being with another person. It felt like a moment where I should've said something or maybe he should've, about how much we loved each other or how we would get married if we survived this. I couldn't say anything eloquently when the only thing keeping me from shitting myself was the fear that the thing outside would smell it. We didn't say a word until we heard a car door slam. Even then, another minute or so passed before he said, "I'm going to look."

"No," I said. I pinned his arm.

"One of us has to," he said.

"What if it sees you?" I said.

"It already knows we're here," he said.

"Be quick. And if it looks back get down."

He popped up. His eyes widened.

"Reynolds?" I said.

"The cop has his light out, he's shining it around the lot. There's nothing there," he said.

I repositioned Reynolds to get a view. An officer in his street blues circled the fence with his flashlight. His car was

parked in the street next to the lot, headlights shining out onto New Jefferson, which was all but empty this time of night. The cop walked further. He plugged his nose. He drew his gun.

"Oh shit," Reynolds whispered.

The cop used his flashlight to stabilize the gun. He pivoted like he'd seen something, though from our vantage, I couldn't. He circled the patch of asphalt inside the fence.

I don't know if Reynolds or I saw it first, but we both started screaming to get the cop's attention when we did. It was like seeing a shark fin in the water. The shadow in the corner behind the cop got darker all at once, as if something swam into it. And then the figure I'd seen rose out of the corner. It passed through the fence as though nothing were there. The cop turned toward Reynolds and me.

"Behind you!" I pointed desperately.

Reynolds muttered, "Oh shit, oh shit, oh shit." The cop looked at us. I wonder now if he had a partner that should've been watching his back. If he had a wife or a husband or kids at home.

The shadow seemed to open, as though it were wearing a cloak, and landed on him. He fired a shot in the air. Dust crumbled from the overpass. The shadow slipped over him. First, he looked like he'd stepped into a dark alley. Then, something tar black went over his chest. His arms and legs flailed. His mouth opened and shut wordlessly. And a few seconds later, his gun clattered on the ground. He was gone.

The thing looked at us again. The smell came back into the room. It was somehow sending it into our apartment. Reynolds fell back off the bed. "Shit, shit, shit."

"Reynolds!" I said. I swung my cast over onto the sheets. The pain in my leg was tremendous. Without the Vicodin to pad it, I had to fight to stay conscious. He ran.

He'd abandoned me. Why would he leave? Where was he going? I twisted the sheets and rubbed my thumb along the seams. I felt as though I were sinking. The smell thickened. I wanted to gag. I turned back out the window and I could see that the shadow had gotten closer, moving out onto New Jefferson Street. It cast its four shadows again, and the tip of the one going forward nearly brought it the rest of the way across the street when Reynolds piled back into the bed. He shined a mag light onto the thing. It depressed where the light hit and pulled back.

He handed me the flashlight. "I'm going to see if I can find more," he said.

I was too surprised to speak. Even if I wasn't, I don't know that I would have anything to say. I did my best to cut the thing off from the street. It retreated under the overpass. The smell dialed back with it, though it didn't completely dissipate. Reynolds came back with another flashlight, the small one we'd used to chase the mouse that had gotten under the stove.

"It's got something to do with the light," Reynolds said. "It can't pass the light."

"What is it?"

"I don't know, but I have to go out there," he said.

"Are you fucking crazy? It ate that cop," I said. How could he even be thinking about confronting this thing?

"He was protecting us," he said. "We owe him."

"He's gone. There's nothing left. It's a gun and a flashlight on the ground," I said. "I can't walk. I need you." I felt terrible as I said it. I'd worked out a system where I could hop from room to room. I couldn't go far or fast, but I could feed myself and make it to the bathroom.

"You're right. You're right. It fucking ate him. What is it?"

I don't have any answers now, even with the sun up. I don't know if I should sleep or not. Reynolds had to go to work. I don't feel safe, but right now, I shouldn't.

2/22/15 (SLIGHTLY LATER MORNING)

I love my fourth-floor neighbor's cat, Joseph. He's cute. He's fun. He will chase a laser pointer for my endless amusement. Today, he has been mewling all day. I don't know what's wrong with him. Maybe he saw the thing. I remember Lisey mentioning that he'd been an outdoor cat before they moved to the city. It doesn't matter. If he doesn't shut up and let me sleep, I'll kill him, and every other pet in the building. They're all going crazy.

2/23/15 (SUNSET)

Reynolds brought home six flood lamps and a two-by-four to mount them to the window. He wanted to fasten it in there. But three cop cars were parked beside the fence, and cops were casing the lot for evidence. They'd closed the street. Which made sense. One of their own had gone missing here. Yellow caution tape blocked off everything.

The cops had followed up with Reynolds and he'd lied, saying he'd seen a hooded figure and dialed 911. He said he'd fallen asleep after that and didn't mention me. If we set up those lights, we would be even more suspicious. But who would believe that it was a shadow monster?

2/24/16

The Neighborhood Gazette website posted three stories of interest today. The first was on the pros and cons of demolishing the overpass. The pros were that drivers commuting into the city from the suburbs would save at least five minutes a day. That was literally all of the pros. Or, I guess, that was all of the pro, because there was just one. The cons were that it would be harder for our neighborhood to reach the station, that we'd have to deal with three years of destruction, and that we'd loved the design. Some fancy pants wrote in saying that the overpass had a gothic build, with little frilly stones. It looked like literally every other overpass I'd ever seen.

The second item of interest: there had been an upswing in the number of pets that had disappeared recently. *The Gazette* advised that all owners keep their pets on leashes until the problem is identified and resolved. The writer suspected coyotes. In Boston.

I know what the problem is.

The third was a profile of the missing cop, Officer Spalonsky. He had a wife and two kids. He played in a Duckpin Bowling league and mouth trumpeted to War's "Low Rider."

2/26/15 (MID AFTERNOON)

I've had phantom shadow syndrome since, and the construction project's been delayed. The cops have followed up with Reynolds twice, but I think at this point they believe he doesn't know anything. They came up to talk to me, too, and I told them that I was on Vicodin for my leg and that I was seeing bugs that Reynold wasn't. It was true and they left me alone.

I'm seeing the thing out of the corner of my eyes, though. I know it's not really there, but whenever there's any shadow, I remember the way it had formed out of the ground beneath Officer Spalonsky. I wish I'd put that article down and ignored his Facebook page with the messages begging him to come home soon. I obsess about the kids and the blonde woman in his profile picture.

The same thing happened after we caught that mouse. We'd used an adhesive trap. The mouse had somehow made it to the center of the pad before the glue snared it. It gnawed off its front left leg and then leapt toward the edge. Its bloody shoulder stuck to the trap. We wanted to be humane, and we were going to drop the twitching lump into the toilet, but Reynolds read that the water might free it, so we wrapped it in three shopping bags. As it thrashed, Reynolds finished it with a hammer.

I caught glimpses of it scurrying in the periphery of my vision for months after that. This time, Reynolds and I were responsible for the death of a man. For orphaning two children. For widowing his wife. We killed him.

2/28/15 (MORNING)

The police left last night. Reynolds says they must think we know something, or that maybe they suspect us. I don't think they do, though. Or at least, rather than us, they suspect him. I can't think about it. If he goes to jail, if I lose him. I can't. We didn't do anything. The shadow ate Officer Spalonsky. We didn't want it to happen. We wanted to be saved.

After the cops cleared out, we set our lights up and then Reynolds brought me down to our fourth-floor neighbors' for dinner. Caroline is a great lady, and her partner Lisey has been away on business for the week. Reynolds suggested that we go and I could get some company, too. It would be no issue for him to get me down just one flight of stairs. It might do us good. Of course, we wouldn't mention the shadow. We'll have spaghetti with meat sauce—the smell has been torturing me since this morning—and pleasant conversation.

And everything was going fine for like two fucking minutes. But when Caroline opened her door, Joseph ran like he'd never run before. Reynolds tried to block him with a leg, but Joseph wriggled through Reynolds' legs in the liquid way cats do. With me in his arms, Caroline couldn't get past Reynolds.

"Shit," she said. "I've got to go after him. Put her down and help me." She'd cut her hair short and wore clothes from the consignment store, and I'd never seen her in a bra. The world wouldn't cow her into doing its bidding. She grabbed it by its bootstraps and put it in its place.

Reynolds ran me into their living room, each bounce jarring where the bones should've been meeting in my leg and dropped me on the couch by the window facing the lot. He smashed down the stairs after them.

I was facing the kitchen, and I could see that Caroline had turned the heat up on the sauce, and it was starting to bubble and hiss. It was going to boil over. There was a rolling chair next to the couch. I tried to lasso it with a pillow, but I knocked it further away. I tried again, but I almost fell.

I hopped over to the chair on one leg. When I grabbed the armrests, it spun away from me, and for a moment I tottered before I found my center. I got a better grip on the chair this time and lowered myself into it. I saved the sauce, but I could tell by the way Reynolds hunched his shoulders when they came back up that they hadn't saved the cat. So much for a relaxing dinner. At least our lights held off the shadow for another night. It seemed to be getting less aggressive as time went on. Like it was giving up. Or maybe it had another victim. Another death on our hands.

Oh, and Caroline complained about her downstairs neighbors. Something about their apartment smelling like rotten eggs.

3/1/15

I can't breathe. I can't stop crying. Joseph wasn't dead. I don't know where he went or what he was doing. Aren't animals supposed to have a sixth sense? They're supposed to be attuned to the natural world. That's why they'd all gotten to higher ground during that tsunami a few years ago. Not this stupid fucking cat. I'm writing this, breaking the cast off, and then I'm going down there myself.

Reynolds and I were sitting on the bed, safe with the lights pinning the shadow until they finally started demolishing the Roland Overpass, and I let my eyes wander out the window and saw Joseph skulking around the fence, like he was looking for a way in. And it's my fault. I shouldn't have pointed him out to Reynolds. It was like I said, "There's Joseph," and Reynolds was half dressed already.

"Where are you going?" I said as he pulled a t-shirt over his head.

"That's our neighbors' cat." He pulled up his jeans.

"So tell our neighbor. Don't go out there," I said, knowing that that was exactly what he would do. Character is destiny, and he was the kind of person who tried to save things. I would like to be, too. Wouldn't we all? But we shouldn't. We should be selfish and tribal. We should be safe.

He threw on his jacket and shrugged the furry part around the neck tight to keep out the cold. "I'll bring a flashlight. I'll be fine."

I should've stopped him. There had to be a way. Maybe if I took off my clothes and jiggled. Maybe if I had just been able to say something persuasive enough to let him know how much more he meant to me than the stupid fucking cat. I could live with the mouse's blood. The cat's blood. Even the cop's blood. Not Reynolds', though. I couldn't let him die because I spotted that cat.

Reynolds did what Reynolds would do, though. He knocked on the door to the fourth-floor neighbors' and when they didn't answer, he went out. I watched as he jogged across the street, flashlight in hand. He climbed the fence slowly and carefully. He propped the flashlight in between the links to protect himself. He hopped over and started making kissy noises at Joseph.

The detestable thing didn't come to Reynolds as he knelt and cooed.

I saw the shadow long before Reynolds did. I had a bird's eye view. It formed in the corner opposite him. Joseph ran to a third corner and couldn't get out. The three made a triangle.

Reynolds moved slowly, circling himself with his flashlight, making sure to shine beneath his feet every few seconds. I grabbed a flashlight myself and pointed it toward the shadow, hoping to use the light to blast it out of its miserable experience. It wasn't strong enough though. The thing sunk back down on its own.

Reynolds surprised me when he dashed toward the cat. He startled Joseph enough to catch him off guard, too. Reynolds scooped the cat up. All he had to do was get back over the fence and into the light. The shadow seemed to sense that, too. It materialized in the center of the asphalt, cutting Reynolds off from the floodlights blasting down from our window.

I tried to angle them further into the fenced off area, but Reynolds had fastened them in too well.

Reynolds swung his flashlight like a pendulum. He didn't try to confront it head on. He was smarter than that. The two of them stared each other down. One more day and my cast would've come off. I could've been down there.

The figment spread out four shadows of its own. They slid out from underneath it one at a time, like the blades of a Swiss army knife coming out in different directions. Reynolds' hand began to shake. He had to come toward the light. I tried to yell for him to come toward it. To come toward me.

He backed himself against the fence. Then the thing turned back and looked at me. That terrible smell came back, like rotting eggs. It was doing this to hurt me because I'd seen it. Because I'd given it a witness, when all it had wanted was to be alive and unseen. To live peacefully under its overpass, and the city had decided to destroy it, and its revenge was to destroy us.

Reynolds tried to make another fast move. He kept the flashlight pointing behind him as he scrambled over the fence. Joseph scratched to get free and threw off Reynolds' balance. Reynolds dropped him and fell. The shadow slipped through the fence and stood over Reynolds. Its four other selves stretched out.

"Leave him alone," I yelled. If it heard me, it didn't show it.

It waited for Reynolds to turn toward me before it took him.

I had to watch. As the tar black covered him. He mouthed the words, "Stay there." And then he was gone.

I love Reynolds.

I guess it should be loved him now.

But he doesn't tell me what to do. I brushed away the broken pieces of cast scattered on the floor. I've gotten good at hopping on one leg over the last few days.

Wish me luck.

Jailbreak

WARDEN CAROL CARDENSKI propped her feet up on a wicker ottoman on Grandma's porch. The nagging pain in her knee had finally passed, and it was one of those glorious early spring days when the sun beaming down felt like love on your skin. The smell of freshly cut grass wafted up from the yard. She swayed back and forth in a white rocking chair, leaning on a pillow her grandmother had sewn [that burned in the fire in 1986]. The lemonade in her glass was freshly squeezed, and her early retirement didn't seem so bad now. Forget the thousand prisoners in the super-max. The new warden's name had slipped her mind, but she was sure they would do fine.

She'd led a retinue of guards down to the basement, and they'd taken care of the thing down there.

[Carol.]

She stretched her arms back, inhaled peace, exhaled stress. The lemonade was fine. The only thing that was missing was a dog.

As she thought it, two dogs zig-zagged up the front walk. The first, Kiki **[she should be in Connecticut, not Pennsylvania]**, was a miniature Schnauzer with a white snout and black fur around her eyes that made her look like a cartoon thief. The second dog, Bernardo, was her grandmother's Jack Russel Terrier who always managed to steal food from Mom's plate and, curiously, never went after anyone else's. **[He burned with that pillow.]**

The dogs chased each other, nipping at one another's heels as Carol laughed. A small boy followed. Her boy, Tommy, as he was at seven or eight. **[Tommy's still mad and you won't apologize, you stubborn thing.]** He was giggling, and it took her back to the time when she'd roll around on the floor for hours, making silly noises just to see him smile, before things had gotten so complicated.

Kiki jumped into her lap first, then Bernardo. The two jockeyed for position, then settled. Tommy padded up the steps after them. "Did you see me, Mom? I almost caught them." He smiled, two front teeth half grown in. **[He didn't lose them at the same time.]** Carol took another drink of lemonade: the perfect mix of sugar, water, and lemon juice. Carol never got it right, but Grandma never missed.

"You want a lemonade?" she asked her boy as she poured him a glass.

Tommy gulped it down and smiled again. The sun glinted off his perfect, grown-in white teeth. **[He never brushed that well.]**

She needed to reapply sunscreen on Tommy and herself.

There wasn't any on the side table. And then there was. It had always been there.

[Something is wrong, Carol. Wake up.]

She picked up the tube. It had the right consistency, the soft skin of the new tubes indenting where the paste slid under her fingers. The color—a sedate blue—was perfect. The words were wrong, though. Something that resembled text was scrawled in the right spots, the right color, but not actual words. She squinted and didn't get any clearer. Something was wrong.

[Yes. Now look out past the yard.]

Kiki jumped up and licked Carol's ear. The dog loved wax. No matter how much time Carol spent with a Q-Tip, Kiki managed to find more. The dog's tongue tickled, wrestling a giggle out of Carol.

Tommy poured himself another glass of lemonade, using two hands to maneuver the pitcher and still not getting it all in the cup. "Cookies!" he yelled.

[It's trying to distract you. Remember the sunscreen.]

A plate of cookies fresh from the oven, chocolate chips still gooey, took the sunscreen's place next to her lemonade on the side table. Carol picked one up with two fingers, trying not to smudge her hands with the melted chocolate. She took a bite.

Heaven. As good as the lemonade. Maybe better. She stuffed the rest of the cookie into her mouth. Then a second.

Tommy scarfed down four. The sugar rush would drive Dale mad, but kids needed to be kids.

Panic stabbed at her. The diabetes. Her sugar would be spiking if she didn't take some insulin soon. All at once relaxation rolled over her. Like the pain in the knee, the diabetes was gone here.

[Look past the yard.]

"Is that my Carol?"

Grandma! Carol had longed to hug her grandmother for so many years. For Grandma to meet her boy. Footsteps approached.

Tommy jerked away as she fixed his hair.

This was impossible.

After the fire, Carol had told herself that her grandmother had moved to Santa Fe. In her dreams, Grandma would come back for a visit, and Carol wouldn't find her at the restaurant. She'd go to the airport to pick Grandma up, but Grandma never streamed out with the other passengers. The dreams only stopped after she'd accepted what happened. It'd been 35 years, and she couldn't go back. Grandma was dead.

Kiki poofed out of existence. Bernardo transformed to what he looked like after the fire—fur singed off, leaving black skin and an exposed liver. She screamed as she tossed the dog carcass off her lap. Tommy was a man again, and he grimaced when he saw her.

She looked past her boy, past the walk. **[Yes!]** Beyond the wintergreen boxwood shrubs, there was nothing. A void of the deepest darkness. The sky ended, too. The sun beat down in a blue square above her, but there was nothing beyond it.

A hand grabbed her shoulder. Grandma. "You can't wake up yet, Carol. We're not finished."

The smell of burnt flesh overpowered the fresh-cut grass and steaming cookies. Warden Carol Cardenski popped up. The ottoman toppled. Grandma's funeral had been closed casket, but this Grandma looked as Carol had imagined. The fire had left a mohawk of white hair, black skin sliding off to show a white skull, eyes melted, and holes burnt through her cheeks, revealing the pink gums and white teeth beneath.

"You're not her," the warden said.

Grandma laughed, a discordant, deep sound, echoing around her insides like a broken piano. "You left the hair straightener plugged in, Carol."

Her legs went weak. She grabbed the closest wicker chair to keep herself up. That fear had niggled in the back of her mind for so long, but the investigator had declared the fire electrical.

"You did this." Grandma pushed a finger between the charred flesh of her cheek and the bone, stretching it.

Grandma hadn't been like this. [**Yes!**] The parasite had gotten inside her.

"Let me out," the warden said.

FOR A SECOND, she was back in control of her body. It felt like she'd broken out of a night terror. She blinked, the old turn-it-off-and-then-on-again, as she tried to get her head on straight. Her body was in the dome in the center of the cells of E Ward, and Associate Warden Andy was on the ground in a downward dog position. Except his head shouldn't have been able to bend in that direction. Oh God. The seat of his pants was wet with shit, and the smell floated up. Andy was dead.

Outside of the dome, the cell doors were open. And the prisoners were flocking toward the unattended exit. What had she done? What else had it done while it was her?

She pressed the talk button on her walkie. "We have a big problem. Code red. Anyone who can read me. Code red."

She ran toward the stairs, and it felt like someone had hit her in the head with a two-by-four.

CAROL PROPPED HER FEET on a hotel room bed, covered in rose petals. The nagging pain in her knee had finally passed. It was a fine day. The sunshine came through the balcony door and bristled with what felt like love. **[It's February and salt has jaundiced the snow.]**

Marvin Gaye was singing about getting it on in the background. Carol sat upright. **[Good! Good, remember.]** She hadn't been at a hotel in years.

That asshole, Cade Tomlinson, had bought the prison. Thanks to the COVID recession, the old owners had to sell. They were horrible, too, but they'd at least respected the thing in the basement. When she'd told Cade about it, he'd laughed.

[Keep going.]

Her velvet robe—the only thing she had on—caressed her skin.

Tomlinson had given her her walking papers, and he'd planned on letting it into gen. pop, where it could swap bodies as much as it wanted. Catching it would be like a game of three-cup monte.

Someone unlocked the room's door.

"Not now, Grandma," Carol said.

But the man in the doorway was not her grandmother. His soft eyes pierced hers, his hair the perfect amount of unkempt. His open shirt revealed a six pack, and she couldn't help herself—her mouth watered. She wanted to lick whipped cream off those abs.

"I've been thinking about you, Warden," he said. His voice was soft and sexy. He rolled a cart with a bottle of champagne in a bucket of ice to the bed.

He reached, slowly, and brushed her hair behind her ears. He cupped her face. His eyes sparkled.

She trembled.

[This isn't real.]

No. It wasn't. And even if it was, she was married, had been for 27 years, and neither of them had strayed too far.

"He doesn't need to know," the man said, eyes smoldering. "When was the last time you did something just for you?"

Dale wasn't a bad husband. Thick around the waist now, but so was she. He always made sure she got hers. He worked, helped with Tommy. She loved him and he loved her, but it wasn't an exciting, dance-all-night, tell-anyone-who-will-listen kind of love anymore. Life with Dale was more like a warm sweater on a cold day but compared to what her sister had with that asshole Lyle, Carol had it good.

Still, it took nearly all of her willpower to push the dream man away.

He pulled her hand onto his meaty chest. God, it felt nice.

"It's okay," he said. "You can enjoy this."

[It's not real.]

"Neither are your dreams. Do you know that your husband thinks of you the way you think of him? Your brother? Your sister? Your children? You think you know but you haven't plumbed their depths, looked into the soft, dark spots. Everything in your life is a fantasy, assembled from incomplete information by a slowly scrambling piece of electrified meat." He uncorked the champagne bottle with a pop. White suds leaked out of the mouth. "Why not indulge?"

She let him kiss her, his warm wet tongue exploring. His body thrust against hers. They fell against the bed. [Carol, it's not real. You need to wake up.]

His weight pressed down on her. She pushed him off and rolled out of the bed. Rose petals fell behind her. "What's going to happen if I open the room door? Or I step out onto the balcony?"

The man's eyes narrowed. "All of this to deny yourself?" [Yes! Carol, yes!]

He followed her, wrapped his arms around her. The hug transformed into a vise when she tried to back away.

She broke the champagne bottle on the hotel end table. "Sorry, handsome," she said. But this wasn't real. She thrust the broken shards into his stomach. It was a shame to destroy those perfect abs, even if in a fantasy.

He groaned and fell back onto the bed, trying to staunch the bleeding with his hand.

She tried the door. The knob rattled, but it was a decoration, not a tool. She squinted at the rest of the room, looking for the loose thread to unravel her prison.

The man pressed the satin sheets against his wound, reddening them with blood.

The balcony doors were fastened shut too. The view beyond—a beautiful beach bathing in sun—was painted between the panes. She grabbed the ice buckets and swung, breaking a hole in the door, revealing the great nothing behind it.

"I'm coming out now," she announced. She reached her hand through the hole, into the chilly abyss.

THIS TIME SHE WAS in the basement, Chief Holloway covering his face with a handkerchief next to her, kneeling in front of the mummified remains of the man the parasite had lived in. The chief rolled the corpse from its side to its back with a pen.

"How long did you say he's been down here?" he asked. His white mustache masked his lips as they moved up and down.

She reached for the wall, anything really, to keep her balance. Switching in and out of the parasite's world disoriented her, as if she'd done a backflip underwater without plugging her nose.

"I need something if I'm going to smooth this over. The feds are on their way. Cade Tomlinson is on the horn, screaming mad. The governor wants to know why you released the prisoners. The DA wants to press charges," Chief Holloway said. "But let's talk about the corpse first."

"Kill me," she said. A wave of dizziness hit her. That thing was taking her under again. "Before it can—"

———

THIS TIME, THE THING burrowing its way through her mind sent her to her own living room. The stack of unread *Fine Gardening* magazines reached as high as the armrest of her threadbare polyester easy chair. Paul Hollywood awarded someone a handshake on *The Great British Baking Show*. Kiki snored gently on Carol's lap. **[It's not real.]**

"I know," she muttered. She stood up, sending Kiki hopping onto the carpet. The parasite hadn't bothered with taking away the pain in her knee in this fantasy. "You're going to have to do better than this," she yelled.

"What, honey?" Dale yelled from the kitchen. The smell of steak sizzling wafted in from the kitchen, followed by the potatoes in the oven. Marrying a man that could cook was the best decision she'd ever made. But this was an illusion, and she needed to find the dangling thread so she could unravel it.

Behind her, the doorbell rang.

"You expecting someone?" Dale yelled from the kitchen.

[Don't answer the door. It's a trick.] The screen door creaked, and she scoffed. In the real world, that door stayed locked at all times. You couldn't stop a crime of determination, but you could stop a crime of opportunity with a plastic lock.

The front doorknob turned. She braced herself for her dead grandmother. For her dream man. For whatever fantasy came next.

Tommy walked through the door. Her boy. He looked

thicker now, like he was eating well and had kicked the compulsion to exercise constantly. [It's not him.] His smile—the real one, not the one he forced for photos—lit up his face. "The door was open, so I came in."

"Is that Tommy?" Dale yelled from the kitchen. [But he didn't come out. Because the monster from the basement wants to lock you away. Dale wouldn't stay in the kitchen if Tommy came home.]

"Tommy?" Carol asked. It had been three years. He'd gone to California with Melissa in his ear, whispering. He was waiting for Carol's apology when he owed her the apology.

Every time Dale said they should call, send a birthday card, she'd said the same thing. The ball was in his court. He'd told her not to call, and heaven forbid she went against the little prince's wishes. But God, March 5th these last three years, it had been a Herculean feat for her not to pick up the phone. And here he was. [You know it's not real.]

The dull ache she pretended wasn't there sharpened.

"Mom," he said. He rubbed his thigh through his jeans. Whether he was 22 months or 22 years old, that gesture had stuck with him.

Who cared whose court the ball was in?

[This isn't real. Tommy is in California. He's not thinking about you.]

Shut up. She knew that on the outside, the feds would be arriving. They'd have questions. Who was the man who'd been kept in the prison basement for the last 120 years? How had the food on his trays been emptying with his body in this advanced state of decay? Cade Tomlinson, the governor, and the DA were all working out a way to put her into prison.

[They won't be able to catch it again. Think about how much damage it could do.]

What could it do? Take one person at a time? And what did the people in the 1900s have that they didn't have now? Just once, this one time, she would do something for her.

[It'll leave a path of destruction.]

"I'm sorry," Tommy said. "I should've never . . . look, it's going to be different now. Melissa was a mistake." Tommy wrapped his arms around her. He still used the Axe body spray, a little too sweet but so familiar.

Forget the monster. Carol melted into her boy.

[It's not going to be real.]

But what was?

Catholic Guilt

I'M LYING IN THE DARK, wondering how my mother managed to convince me to come on yet another one of these family vacations and why I hadn't just taken a wine cooler and sat down at the kid's end of the table, when the music starts in the parlor. Bach's Toccata and Fugue in D minor. The haunted house song. Of course. I want it to be one of my uncles screwing with me. My mom was the oldest and she had me young, so they're actually closer to my age, 23, than to hers, and they used to save their boogers on index cards and chase me around. So I wouldn't put it past them, sneaking down from the bedrooms while their wives try to sleep, and putting on this creepy-ass organ music.

What I don't get is how they'd be willing to freak out their own kids just to scare me. Out of my mom's five brothers, maybe two are decent dads. But even the other three don't want to deal with their beautiful children (whose best genes no doubt come from their wonderful mothers, because no nibbling has seemed to catch any part of the jerkoff gene that infects their fathers) running into their beds and blocking their vacation sex, which I heard one of them bragging to the rest could possibly be oral.

The way the house is laid out, I'm sleeping across the hall from the kitchen. The hall goes down the side of the dining room, which, by Grandma's decree, has a big enough table to sit all 23 of us without a separate kid's table. The dining room connects to the kitchen on one side, and a parlor on the other. There's a swinging door between the kitchen and the dining room and a sliding one at the parlor. The stereo with its spooky-scary Sebastian Bach is on that far end, and my youngest uncle, Alex, has closed every door in the house because his one-year-old Elizabeth, the cutest damn girl in the world, loves doing naked laps but can't reach doorknobs yet. I can either walk down the hallway for the length of an Olympic-sized pool, or I play the game of opening three doors and scare the piss out of myself three times.

The thing is, I don't want anyone with an ounce of my blood in their veins to see me in the gym shorts and tank top I sleep in, and I couldn't turn back in the hallway if someone else were coming to investigate. I'd have to press on and pretend like I don't know what they're thinking. Of course, Janie's daughter (Did you know she was born out of wedlock? The scandal!) doesn't sleep in a nightgown like a proper lady.

So, I go through the first door, into the kitchen, and I leave the light off. My eyes are adjusted to the dark, and if it is an uncle screwing with me, and I come from this side, I might manage to scare him instead.

The kitchen's got a granite island covered in an excessive number of knives. Like, seriously. Whoever stocked this place must have wanted to have enough knives that they could stab every guest with their own individual blade. There is no other possible explanation for a house having so many knives.

I put a hand on the island and follow it to the door to the dining room, and all the time this Johann joker's getting louder. The air conditioning's chilled the tile floor and granite, so I'm getting goosebumps all over. I'm trying to play it in my head like I'm getting closer, and that's why it sounds louder, not that it's being turned up because someone would need to be able to sense me through three closed doors to change the volume as I get closer.

That's when ye olde Catholic programming kicks in, and I'm saying Hail Marys under my breath and thinking about how mad I'll be in the morning for falling back into religion. Forgive me, it's been 13 months since my last regression.

Here's the thing about being raised Catholic: You can be an atheist for a decade, read the complete works of Nietzsche, and defecate on the steps of a Church, but when everything goes to crap, you're back praying to the sweet lord baby Jesus. They programmed you. It starts at age three or so with people teaching you that if you think a set of words, you don't even need to say them aloud, an all-powerful being is going to pop down and intercede on your behalf. That toy you wanted? Yours. The bully from the school bus? Smote. Whatever you want, you say enough Our Fathers and Hail Marys, and it will be yours, and you don't need to do a thing to achieve it. And here I am, in a rented mansion in Cape Cod, with 23 of my mother's ass-hat relatives, praying that it is a living, flesh-and-bones, non-ethereal being who turned on the stereo.

I don't like my odds.

I put my hand on the door to the dining room. It's a butler's door, so the Colonel, a Union general in the Civil War according to our travel agent, could have food in and out as fast as possible while still not having to linger with the help. It can swing all the way open into either room, and it moves at the slightest touch. I peek through the crack, making sure an uncle or something else isn't there to jump out at me, but I can't see much.

I've got a view of the back of the Colonel's chair. There's a dresser that's filled with silverware and fine china on the left. Everything is made of oak, and the corners have been carved into flowery vines and buds. These little flourishes make people like my grandmother, born in Irish Boston, feel like they've made it. There's a silver mirror above the dresser, but I only catch the edge of it, not enough to get the rest of the room in the reflection.

I let the door swing back toward me but stop it from coming back into the kitchen. Who or whatever is working the stereo isn't going to see me.

I hit the door open a little farther. This time, I get three-and-a-half seats, including the head of the table. They're empty. The door that leads from the hallway into that side of the dining room is on the right. It's closed, and I'm glad because if it were open, I'm sure there'd be something going past it in the corner of my eye as soon as I passed it.

I plunge through, into the dining room. I say a Hail Mary. I walk around the table on the opposite side of the door. I want to be as far from any entry point as possible. What I really want is to be safe, curled up in bed, with a sheet, preferably a quilt in this air conditioning, pulled up to my chin. But Bach has gotten even louder, and I'm sure it's not the diminishing number of doorways between me and the stereo. The jumps it's making are too loud.

The doors to the parlor come into view. They're heavy sliders, and I realize that I won't be able to push them open quietly. I wish I was back in bed again, and I tell Jesus—whom I'd like to believe in only as a historical figure—that I'd like his intercession in the matter of the haunted stereo.

I touch the wooden top of each chair as I go by. Running my hand across something smooth, the calm of finished carpentry, soothes me as much as I can be soothed. I wonder why I don't give up. With Bach getting louder, someone else will hear and turn off the damned stereo. Maybe I keep going because if it's my uncles, they will smell my fear in the morning. Maybe I go because my cousins will get woken up, and as much as I hate my uncles, I love their children even more. Maybe I go because I need to know exactly what is working the stereo, and at some level, I believe that if I can prove it is an electronic problem or a manmade disturbance, I can return to my unspiritual life. I don't know why I do the things that I do, and I suspect that the people who believe they do are lying to themselves.

Another Hail Mary. I'm at the sliding doors now. I put my ear to them, and the ever-louder fugue is too loud for me to hear if anything is moving in the room. Or maybe everything is still. I can't tell.

I press my finger into the cracks between the doors. I don't know what I'm hoping to find, what I'm expecting. In chaos there is infinite possibility, but all probability points to this being a prank. I believe that the world is chaos. Maybe it's "believed" now. Past tense.

Here I am, praying, terrified, and opening the door. Was this what my mother was hoping for when she told me this vacation would give me a chance to bond?

The doors creak loudly. In a leather armchair, there is a woman I have never seen before. She doesn't turn at the squeals of the runner. Her hair is short and seems to be blonde and white all at once. Her legs are folded. When I get the doors all the way open, she looks up at me, and I feel as though an ice cube has been stuffed down the back of my shirt. We make eye contact. Hers are green, but as I look into them, I can see the red, white, and blue of the flag blanket hanging over the back of the chair. I can see through her. I'm too afraid to move. I feel as though I'm going to vomit.

"You're not my husband," she says.

I shake my head no. I almost motormouth and tell her that I'm not anyone's husband. Tell her I like her dress. Thank her for allowing my family into her home so graciously. Ask her if she's a big baroque fan. Ask her how this is happening. I have so many things to say that none can get out.

"I haven't seen him in years," she says, wistfully. She rubs at her eye, as though she's been crying. The music is hurting my ears now, but I can hear her perfectly.

"Will you pray with me?" she says.

I nod. What else am I going to do? It's her house. We're just renting it.

She puts her hands on her knees and rocks forward gently. "It takes me a minute to stand up now," she explains. She's transparent, but I feel her like I've never felt anyone. It's like I've jammed a fork into a socket. She manages to climb out of her chair on the third try, and she reaches out for me.

I know from my great-grandparents that I'm meant to put my arm out here, let her grab my forearm and guide her to her destination. I step back instead, and she falls forward. She is gone before she hits the floor. The stereo shuts off on its own. I shiver. Even with the air conditioning blasting, I shouldn't be this cold. I wonder who she was and who I am.

The Urge

THE RAIN DROWNED OUT the chorus of a sugary pop song on the top 40 station as Tony inched his car through the storm. His windshield wipers couldn't get the job done. Neither could his lights. The fog reflected his high beams back at him, so he focused on the two feet of road that he could make out through the enveloping gray.

He rolled to the intersection of Swamp Hill Road and Lover's Lane and came to a complete stop, hands at 10 and 2. Then he craned his neck to check for headlights around the blind curve. His wife would've nagged him about how stopping when there wasn't a stop sign was dangerous, and their daughter would have rolled her eyes because they were having *this* argument again. But he was alone in the car.

Mostly.

He clicked on his blinker and took a right toward the Lover's Lane Bridge. The city had been "planned" around cowpaths. That choice saved a couple of bucks by paving the

ground already flattened by livestock, but cows didn't walk in a grid, which led to roads full of hairpin turns like Lover's Lane. The city didn't even bother with guard rails this far out.

But even in the fog, he'd driven this stretch a thousand times. He made the turn onto the bridge perfectly before he saw the girl in the road. He slammed on his brakes, and the car hydroplaned to a stop a foot from her.

She was maybe 17, long shapely legs that had to be freezing sticking out of that skirt. Her letterman's jacket too thin to stop the rain.

Tony sat there, staring. He should pick her up. To help her out. He could be a good Samaritan, couldn't he? He didn't need to act on the Urge.

He pulled up and rolled down the passenger window. "Need a lift?"

It would be fine. There wasn't a single reason in the world the cheerleader would find out about the body in his trunk.

IN THE CAR, she was even lovelier with her hands folded over her crossed legs. Her blonde hair, straight and dry despite the weather, enthralled him. He tried to keep his nostrils from flaring as he smelled her. She should've smelled like roses. Lilies. Lilacs. Instead, she smelled like a waterlogged corpse.

"Where are you heading?" he asked, injecting his voice with warmth.

She stared out the passenger-side window. He was being pretty darn nice, stopping to pick her up, getting her out of the rain. The least she could do was tell him where to drive her.

"Honey," he said. He pressed his thumb into the groove of

the wooden handle of the switchblade in the cupholder on the driver-side door. Sometimes that helped with the Urge.

She turned to him, bright green eyes glistening, and blinked. "I'm trying to make it to the game." Her mascara ran in the rain.

It was a Friday in late fall, so there might be a football game. His daughter might have mentioned it. He let go of the knife, hands back at 10 and 2. "Away we go," he said. He forced a smile.

"That's swell," she said.

Swell. Weird word. "Are you on the cheer squad?" he asked.

She'd turned back to the window. Ignoring him again. He picked the knife up this time, squeezing the folded blade inside the wooden handle. He imagined flaying her, peeling her skin off like it was a sticker.

Then he put the knife back in the cupholder. There were things he wanted and things he needed. Tony wanted to kill. In order to kill, he needed to stay out of jail. Two missing girls would be too many at once.

"My daughter goes to your school, I think. McKinley?"

She didn't answer again. Her disrespect was a canker sore he couldn't stop pressing his tongue against. Here he was, being a nice guy, and she couldn't even make small talk. The pretty princess high in her castle, ignoring the lowly servant.

"Did you—"

She turned back toward him, and for a second he saw something different. Instead of her face, he saw what it would look like half rotted off, a puddle of muddied flesh sloughing off the white bone of her chin. "I went to McKinley."

That glimpse scared the shit out of him. His hands shook on the wheel. He trained his eyes on the fog-covered road. Rain pelted the roof. The engine purred. He turned off Lover's Lane, onto Main Street.

"What gate should I drop you at?" he asked as he slipped the knife out of the cupholder.

Whatever she was, the Urge wanted to feel the blade of his knife dig through the muscle of her neck until it chipped the bone. He kept glancing at her to see which form she was taking. For now, a regular teenager staring out the window. The blade flicked open.

The knife thwipped toward where she'd been sitting, but she had disappeared. Her letterman's jacket sat in a pile on the seat. From somewhere unseen, she giggled. He spun around to face an empty backseat. He picked up her jacket, fury meeting fear in a queasy mix. How did she disappear like that?

Tony drained a flask of rotgut whiskey before he went back out to Lover's Lane that night. He knew he wouldn't see Miss McKinley again, but he still needed to bury the girl in the trunk. They were probably talking about her at the football game. Would it be too soon for them to give her parents a microphone and let them talk about the way she wore her hair, how she said good morning, and the way her eyes crinkled when she smiled?

He went through two sets of emotions. The Urge came, and he'd spent months, sometimes years, fighting it off. Once in a while, he'd win, and a girl would go off to college far enough away he wouldn't be able to follow her. But more often, and more and more frequently, he'd give in. There'd be weeks of news coverage, searches, vigils. And the worst part was that he'd really cry at all of it. He was at his core a disgusting creature, like his father had said, a hemorrhoid on the ass of life.

But that didn't mean he wanted to go to jail. So, he poured lye on the face of the dead girl, broke her teeth, and buried her in the swamp outside Lover's Lane.

Normally, he'd get a few months reprieve before the Urge came back. He picked up Miss McKinley's jacket when he was done, and he smelled it. She wasn't dead enough.

HE WORKED IN the bursar's office at a small college a half hour away from his town. It was his responsibility to sit stone-faced across from the crying students—begging for extensions, for holds to be lifted off their accounts so they could register for next semester's classes or walk across the graduation stage—and say no.

Depressing work, but after the rush at the beginning of each semester, his only responsibility was to automate the charges for the next semester. So that next week, he did as many Google searches as he could, trying to find the record of a girl that he hadn't killed who died or went missing in his town.

When Google didn't turn anyone up, he logged into his subscription to the town paper and crawled through the digital microfiche. He started in the 50s because she'd said "swell," and then moved into the 60s and 70s.

When he'd made it to the 90s, he went backward through the 40s. Girls had gone missing, but none that looked like her. None that were cheerleaders. And it irked him. He couldn't bring his knife with him into the office, so he squeezed a pink stress ball with "Midnight Breakfast: Finals 2017" on it in faded black letters.

After the newspaper, he went through the virtual tour of the town graveyard, looking for anyone who died in their teens. No news coverage. No grave. What was she?

The bursar herself appeared in the doorway. Voice still raspy from 20 years of cigarettes ten years after she'd quit, she asked, "How're the charges for spring semester coming?"

"Oh, great," he said. He hadn't started, but it never took as long as he pretended. For now, he had bigger fish to fry.

AT HOME, he drank more. Instead of sleeping when he closed his eyes, he saw her faces: the rotted one and the facade. The Urge throbbed in his chest. He snapped at his wife for nothing, yelled at his daughter for not understanding her algebra when it was really quite simple.

His wife rubbed his shoulders as he reclined in his chair. "Honey, is something bothering you?"

"Just work," he said.

"It's okay if you don't want to talk about it, but if you snap at me or our daughter one more time, I'm going to put your balls on a skewer."

There was a pounding in his ears. Sometimes he pictured his wife's face on the body of his girls.

———

HE'D SPENT AN HOUR or so tossing and turning, begging the Urge for a reprieve. When it overpowered him, he snuck out and drove across the Lover's Lane Bridge. He huffed her jacket, hoping that she would feel him.

On rainy nights, he might catch a peek. The red of her jacket through some trees. The blonde of her hair illuminating the darkness. He'd rush to the spot and hear a far-off giggle. The same scent from her jacket was lingering in the woods.

Who was hunting who?

HE STARTED CHECKING the forecast compulsively. The bursar was rambling about changes to the billing for the spring semester in a meeting, and he checked his phone to see if there were any storms coming in.

"Tony, what are you doing?" she asked.

"Oh, sorry," he said.

"You okay?" the bursar asked. "You're late on the automation, and you seem out of it."

"I know," Tony said, unable to shake the disappointment of the sunny forecast. Normally, it would be foggy for weeks this time of year. Storms for days. And here he was, stuck with the sun.

HE THOUGHT HE HEARD the giggling while his daughter performed at her violin recital, and the Urge took over completely. He jumped out of his chair. The legs scraped against the wooden floor as people turned to shush him. His wife grabbed at his pants as he scrambled for the back of the room, where he'd heard the sound.

"Tony," his wife hissed. "Where are you going?"

He ran through the entryway, scanning for Miss McKinley. The rotten scent on her jacket floated on the air, as if carried by a far-off wind. He focused on his breathing to center himself and stepped back into the auditorium, back into a sea of dirty looks.

His daughter, a consummate musician, had continued, though she cried as she played. He wouldn't just kill Miss McKinley. He would torture her.

At work, he fell down another Google rabbit hole: how do you kill a ghost?

It didn't turn up much. For one thing, he didn't know if she was a ghost. She could be a ghoul. A wraith. A zombie. A vampire. A succubus. He didn't have enough info. But he worked toward assembling a one-size-fits-all kit.

He snuck into a church and dipped his switchblade into the holy water stoup near the entrance. From the hardware store, a set of wooden stakes meant for a tent and a mallet to drive them through her heart. From the grocery store, garlic. He had to order the silver knife online. He tossed in a Bible for good measure.

He was rereading his checklist when she knocked on his office door: the red letterman's jacket, the blonde hair. He stared at her, eyes bulging, unable to speak. His kit was stashed in the car. The Urge took the driver's seat.

"Is this the bursar's office?" she asked.

"You think you can ruin my daughter's recital," he yelled. He lunged across the room and grabbed the girl's wrist.

She screamed.

He blinked and saw that the nose was all wrong, too big and slightly crooked. This girl's eyes were a different shade of green.

Footsteps rushed from the office around his. He let go of the girl's wrist, and she rubbed at it. The bursar pushed through. "Tony, what the hell are you doing?"

THE BURSAR PUT him on administrative leave. That night, he didn't even wait for his wife and daughter to go to sleep. He drove off, mid-argument. He rolled his window down on the bridge and shouted for her.

"Honey?"

"Miss McKinley?"

"Swell girl?"

When she didn't answer, he took her jacket out of the glovebox and shoved his face into it, breathing in what was left of her half-rotten scent.

"ADMINISTRATIVE LEAVE?" his wife hissed, still awake and in a robe, when he got home. She stared at him, unrelenting. Her face turned red.

He rubbed the back of his neck. "I, uh, think I may—"

"Stop," his wife said, rage bubbling under her words. "If you can't be a decent father and you can't help pay the mortgage, this will be all. Take your things. Go."

The Urge wanted him to take her. Why the fuck not? But it didn't overpower him the way it did when it came to Miss McKinley. He balled and unballed his hands, felt his breaths, and centered himself before he packed a bag.

He found a residency hotel near the outskirts of town. Three payments behind, but no one had come to take his car yet. His daughter had refused to say goodbye to him. But none of that mattered. It was background noise to the screaming Urge for her. The girl with the living and the dead face. And finally, the forecast called for rain.

Once he finished off Miss McKinley, he could go back to the bursar and tell her he was cured. He could go back to his wife and daughter and plead for forgiveness. They'd welcome him home once the money was back. And maybe this would be the last time the Urge would take over. Letting it take control one last time could be the thing to finally rid him of it.

He inched through the fog again, headlights not making more than a two-foot dent as he approached the bridge. Again, he came to a full stop and then turned on his blinker. He edged out onto the bridge, ready to stop the car. To offer her a ride.

And there she was. Legs tanner, more shapely. Hair a brighter blonde. Rain plastered her blouse against her chest, and he wanted to take a bite out of her boobs. He laughed. Now that he'd lost everything, he finally found her.

He rolled next to her and swung open the passenger-side door. "Get in."

This time, she didn't look away. She glued her green eyes to him as she climbed onto the passenger seat, on her knees, facing him. Instead of buckling in, she reached for him.

She grabbed his ears, turning his head toward her. "Whoa. What the fuck are you doing?"

Her mouth opened. Her cheeks stretched as her jaw kept going down. He tried to turn his head, but she held tight. The skin of her cheeks turned white and then split as her jaw unhinged. Behind the human teeth, there was another layer of sharper, pointed teeth.

He grabbed the holy water knife from the cupholder and flipped it open, one-handed. She jerked his head forward, toward her mouth. He stabbed her throat, steel blade piercing soft skin.

She grunted. He pulled the knife out. She gasped. He had a whole kit in the trunk if that didn't work.

Black bile sprayed out of the hole. It soaked his face and chest, burning. He stabbed again and again as his face sizzled with the gunk. She made noises with each stab. The black stuff melted his eyelids shut, but he heard her fall back. Felt her fingers release his head.

He tried to wipe the fluid from his eyelids. The skin came off with it. The air felt strange on the bits of his eyes where he'd never felt it before. Blood blotched his vision. His muscles blinked, but there was no skin to move. As he dabbed at the gunk, more of his face came off.

She wasn't dead in the passenger seat. Her hands were folded over her crossed legs as she waited. They made eye contact. Then she lunged for what was left of his face.

<hr>

After she pinned "his" confession to his chest, she rolled Tony's car off the bridge. They really ought to put in guardrails.

She walked north, toward another town where a couple of girls had gone missing over the last four months.

Social Experiment

S TAN'S HEAD ACHED like someone had whacked him with a two-by-four. He stretched on the hard surface. His hip felt worse than his head. Above him, a red light blinked. Maggie was next to him, but she didn't have any sheets or blankets. And neither did he. They lay on a stainless-steel floor. He shook his wife's leg. His stomach tightened.

They'd gone to a dinner at the Phillips' house and the Phillipses were teetotalers. They'd served prime rib, rare, with scalloped potatoes. He remembered thinking that this was too fancy for him. He stayed home with the baby, and she worked in the university legal department. She'd actually represented Jenny Phillips in a case for violating Institutional Review Board ethics recently, but Stan couldn't remember the details.

Maggie's eyes opened. Her formal dress, the pink one with the X's showing flashes of brown skin and bra in the back, was rumpled. "What did we do last night?"

The room was about ten feet by ten feet. Like the floors, the walls and ceilings appeared to be stainless steel. There was one light fixture, a red eye in the center winking at them over and over, tinting the steel rectangles. The farthest wall had a pressure-sealed door with a handwheel in the center.

Stan wrestled it. First left, and then right. It wouldn't budge. "Where's Holly?" he asked.

Maggie sat bolt upright. "Where are we?"

"Good morning, Clarks," a robotic voice said.

The two searched for the voice, both settling on the red light above them, which stopped flashing, dropping the room into darkness. "We're transcending the Institutional Review Board and its kindergarten right-wrong ethics. You have been conscripted for a social experiment on how couples deal with adversity. You are our variable group for how interracial couples—specifically white and Indian—respond to deadly situations."

"Dr. Phillips? Jenny?" Maggie squinted up at the light.

"This chamber is completely airtight. Once the experiment begins, we'll reduce the amount of oxygen in the room so there'll be enough air for two people for one-and-a-half hours and enough for one person for three. The door will open in two hours. If one of you is still alive, you'll be permitted to leave."

"One of us?" Maggie asked.

"Yes," the emotionless voice answered. "If one of you does not die within about 90 minutes of the experiment starting, you'll both die. Do you have any questions before we begin?"

"No you fucking don't!" Maggie yelled. She jumped at the red eye, reaching to swat it but falling short.

Stan said, "Alright. This was funny. You had your laugh. Let us out now, Jenny."

"We'll be observing as the experiment progresses. If there are no questions, let's begin."

A set of skinnier steel rectangles in the ceiling slid open, revealing black nozzles underneath. Vacuums whirred on. Air whooshed loud enough to pop Stan's ears. A wave of light headedness knocked him on his ass. Maggie jumped at the ceiling, trying to block one of the nozzles. She batted at it, then fell on the unforgiving metal floor.

The steel rectangles pistoned shut. If Maggie's hand had been there, she'd be missing a couple of fingers.

"Thank you, Clarks. Your sacrifice will provide an invaluable window into how stress impacts interracial relationships."

STAN KNOCKED ON every wall, one after the other, listening for a hollow echo. It wouldn't have mattered with stainless-steel walls, but there had to be another way. He pressed his fingers into the seams, looking for any crevice.

Maggie twisted at the handwheel. "Must be magnetically sealed," she said.

"Did you think *you* could do twisting it after I couldn't?" he asked. Honestly, he wanted to know. Did she think him incompetent? Or that, improbably, she was stronger than he was? He didn't believe in that gender-role bullshit people pushed, but he'd seen how many trips it took her to take in the groceries when he lugged them all in one trip.

"I had to be sure," she said. She sat down, back against the door.

"You're wasting our air, exerting yourself somewhere I already have," he said.

"Did you find any weak spots?" she asked.

He made his way back to the center of the room and laid down. "Yeah. A ton of them. I was waiting for you to ask before we escaped."

"I feel like you think it's my fault we're trapped in here when you get snippy with me."

The I-feel statements. Marriage counseling strikes again. "You're right," he said, but only because she was. If they didn't have Holly, this would've been so much easier. He could picture a different world where they'd snuggle into each other's arms, reminiscing as the air supply dwindled. But they couldn't give up with a baby waiting on the other side.

She slid over to him from the door. "So, you're sorry?"

"Yes, I'm sorry," he said. Another waste of air. He put his head on her lap. They'd sat on the couch like this so many nights, watching the Netflix show of the week. Sometimes he'd get out his sketchpad and doodle one of the characters from the show.

"Do you remember the night we met?" she asked.

"No," he said and badly suppressed a grin.

She smacked him on the arm.

Neither of them said anything out loud, but Stan liked to think that Maggie was walking through the memory with him.

They'd met before the advent of Tinder, a time when people who met online still made up elaborate cover stories to conceal that fact. Stan and Maggie had met the old-fashioned way, blackout drunk at a bar.

He wished that it had been more romantic, but their college rented out a bar for senior week, and they'd both been on the dance floor, in each other's gravitational pull when, "I Won't Give Up" by Jason Mraz came on. So they fell into each other's arms, strangers. The slow dance escalated into making out, which escalated into her friends pulling the two of them apart.

The next night at the next senior-week bar, he grabbed an extra champagne flute for her for the toast, thinking to apologize if he'd taken advantage. She'd grabbed one for both of them, too, and they'd made out again—this time, sober enough that her friends were only upset, not worried. His friends slapped him on the back. This time, he got her number. She had an internship in New York City in the same building where he would be working on the maintenance crew. Kismet.

The red light blinking above them stopped again, plunging the world into darkness. "You have 105 minutes remaining until the door opens. And 150 minutes of air remaining for one person."

A panel in the center of the floor slid open, jostling them off of it. A steel table ascended. One corner was stained brown. Knife cuts were grooved in it.

Stan grabbed at his chest to keep from wheezing.

Maggie went to the table and scratched at the blood. "I think it's real," she said.

Stan shook his head and forced the words out. "You know, it's going to have to be me."

She shoved him. "Can't we just take a minute."

"It's the logical thing to do."

"I don't want to talk about that."

"You're the breadwinner. Holly and I, we couldn't . . ." He didn't finish his sentence. He didn't want to say it. When they'd applied for mortgages, the broker sat them down and explained that with Stan's student debt and less than three years of receipts for his graphic design business, he was a negative $45,000 asset if he were to be on the loan.

"My life insurance policy is worth a million dollars," she said.

He'd forgotten about that. His was for a hundred grand. With a million dollars, he could pay off his loans and get a house. But it wouldn't buy Holly a new mother or unbreak his heart. He wanted to smash that blinking red eye. "Not if I murder you."

"I'm not sure it would be murder, given the circumstances," she said. "We were coerced."

"You're the lawyer," he said.

"But listen, why are we accepting what that thing says?" She got up and went to the handwheel again. This time she traced her finger around the crevices of the door.

"You think Jen is lying?" He knew Jennifer was a doctor and hated having her name shortened. But given that she'd kidnapped him and his wife for an experiment, he didn't exactly feel compelled to treat her with respect. "Old Jenny from the block?"

"I think we need to walk through some of this before we . . . you know."

"Okay." He flipped the camera the bird.

Maggie cuddled up to him, her feet on his thigh. He didn't know how she could cuddle at a time like this. His stomach tightened like someone had put it in a vise.

"What evidence do we have that there's actually only 150 minutes of air in this room?"

The room was getting warmer, stuffy. No matter how deeply he breathed, his lungs didn't fill all the way.

"If I could get precise measurements, I could determine the volume of the room. But I'd need to know more about the air levels." She examined the walls, not tapping on them like he did but tracing their outlines with her eyes.

Math had always been a challenge. He could do addition and subtraction in his head quickly, but he'd taken a stats class to avoid calc in college. Figures were her thing. "Is there a way to figure out based on the size of the room?" Then he slapped his leg. "You must feel the way the room is changing."

"No," she said.

"One of us needs to die," he said. He pictured four squares with the possible outcomes.

"What about the babysitter?"

Lizzy! Teenagers didn't stay late for free. Her parents would get involved. They'd call the police, who would find Jen and rescue them. "She could've already dialed 911."

"Who knows how long we were unconscious," she said.

"So, we just need to hang tight, right?" His stomach rumbled.

"Yeah," she said. She finished her circuit around the walls. "Do you think we need to factor in our physical exertion, too? Like, if we breathe more, we'll take up more air."

Of course they did. "I don't want to think about this anymore. Tell me something about yourself that you've never told me before," he said.

He knew so much. That she'd cheated to win the spelling bee in third grade. That in sixth grade, because her parents wouldn't buy her any, she'd sometimes chew the gum from under the desk if it was still warm. How her parents wouldn't let her date in high school, so she'd invented a secret boyfriend three months before prom, and she'd had to fake a breakup and pretend to be sad at the dance.

"You know the Mickey Mouse clock, the one I had as a kid?"

Of course he did. Her dad had a little too much one day and smashed it. When Stan heard the story, he did some research and found one on eBay.

"It broke my heart when you replaced it. The thought was so sweet, but the new clock didn't close the hole, or whatever you thought it might do. Every time I look at it, I see him breaking it."

He nodded and absorbed the information. "I was thinking you'd say something more cute. Like you used to 'borrow' the neighbors' scooter when they left it in the driveway."

"Is that your secret?" she asked.

"Yeah," he said.

"Doesn't count."

"Why not?"

"Because you already told me that, like at least 15 times. Every time we see those Byrd Scooters downtown, you're compelled to confess," she said. She traced his thumb nail with hers. He loved her so much.

"So, I've got to try again?" he asked. He really should've thought of an answer for the question before he'd asked it. "My brother, Harry, remember how he had cancer?"

She looked at him, annoyed.

"The first time, when we were kids, I used to think that Ginger Ale was specially designed to stimulate appetite. Like secretly. Because when we'd visit him in the hospital, I'd always have one and get so hungry afterward. I thought it had to be that way to counteract the nausea of the chemo."

The red light in the ceiling stopped blinking. "You have 95 minutes until the door opens and 130 minutes of air remaining for one person. As I've been monitoring your conversation, I would like you to know that I have picked up Holly and paid the babysitter."

The microphone clicked. On the other end, a baby babbled, "Dadadadadada."

Maggie squinted at him. "Is that her?"

He'd had this weird sensation since Holly was born. Even when he was holding her, if he heard another baby cry, he'd think it was her. He'd hear phantom cries, too, as she slept. SIDS scared him so much, he got up every time. "Yes."

"I assure you, Clarks, she'd prefer to have one parent than none." The red light began flashing again.

A steel box rose out of the center of the table with a hydraulic hiss. It opened to reveal a row of five butchers' knives.

"Jesus fucking Christ," Stan yelled. He hopped up, sending Maggie sprawling. He stalked toward the closest wall, wound up to punch it, and then stopped himself. A broken hand wouldn't make this better.

"Stan, the air," she said. The room continued its one-way journey, stuffier and stuffier.

"Fuck!" he yelled. He ripped open his shirt, buttons clinging off the stainless steel. "It has to be me."

"We're not doing that," Maggie said. She put a hand on his shoulder, gentle, reassuring.

"Maggie, we have to. One of us has to survive this. For Holly." It would've been so much easier if they didn't have a kid. In his worst imaginings, the ones where Holly and Maggie died in an accident, he'd kill himself, too. Because what was he without them? He made a thousand bucks a month on his graphic design business, not enough to live on.

They'd talked about who would die first. When you'd gotten past the five-year mark, it seemed natural. Maybe they should've even done it sooner. He wanted to die first. She wanted to live until 75 and skip the decline their parents were going through.

"I can't kill you," she said, voice quiet, stilted. Her hand slipped off his shoulder.

"Do you think I could kill you?" he asked. They'd wrestle in the bedroom sometimes, a prelude, so he knew he could pin her down, but then what?

She grabbed her arms, trying to steady herself from shaking. "I thought she was our friend."

The knives reflected the red light flashing above them.

"I'm sorry. I don't know what useful data this could get anyone. But I've read about the Milgram Experiment. The Stanford Prison Experiment. The experiments the Nazis did in the concentration camps. But she's going to kill us both or kill one of us. And listen," his voice broke, but he kept talking, "I can't make a living the way you can."

"I can't talk about this." Maggie walked into a corner.

"I'm sorry, but the clock is ticking. We have to," he said. He followed her across the room.

A wave of anger hit him. This woman, this incredible person, would be gone. Or he'd be gone from her. He slapped the steel wall. The reverberation ached in his fingers, but it gave him a measure of relief, physical pain overriding the mental.

"What kind of old people do you think we would've been?" she asked.

"I'm grumpy now," he said.

"I always pictured myself gardening once I retired, getting really good at it, too, like my mom. Maybe I'd hire some neighborhood kids to weed."

He pictured her in a floppy hat, holding a spade. "That was my first job. Nine years old, and my mom had me going around the neighborhood, helping out the little old ladies," he said.

"That's why I'd do it. I wanted to meet a little you. And see old you yell at him for missing a spot," she said.

"I always thought I'd volunteer once I got things together. Go to the hospital and do caricatures of the sick kids, you know?"

The room went black. "You have 80 minutes until the door opens. One-hundred minutes of air remain."

The microphone clicked.

Stan took off his belt. "It has to be me," he said. He grabbed a knife and held it again his wrist, unable to cut.

"Stan, no," she said.

He shoved the handle in her hand and put his wrist against the blade. It nicked him.

"You can't," she said. "I should be the one to die."

He backed away. "What?" The truth was that not only was she the breadwinner, but the better parent, too. Sure, he was home with the baby, but so much of his day was setting Holly in her crib and wandering away to draw. Whether she went to sleep or screamed for an hour, he dedicated the time to his art.

"You're in Texas for me, to be near my parents," she said. "If I die, you get a million dollars, and you're free. You hate it here. You can sell the house, too."

He did hate Texas. He didn't want to be anywhere that tried to pass laws about who could use what bathroom but then got furious over banning assault rifles. Back in New England, you could assume that anyone you talked to under 50 would pretty much agree with you on politics, but here it was a coin toss who would start spouting off about communism and Second Amendment rights if politics came up.

"I can't raise her without you," he said. They'd read the parenting books together. Done all the research. He executed the game plan, but he didn't know if he could make it on his own.

She turned away from him. "I couldn't be home with her that much." She went over to the red light in the ceiling. "Isn't this enough for your results? Seeing us fall apart? We're arguing over which one of us should die, Dr. Phillips. What else could you want to see?"

"She's not going to answer," he said. He rubbed at his forehead. His headache doubled in pain. The breaths weren't filling his lungs.

"Why us? Do you think interracial couples are that different?"

A thought struck him, and he laughed. If his uncles had been in this situation, there wouldn't be any question what would happen. For all their talk about a woman being like a flower, they'd beat their wives to death in less than an hour.

"What's so funny?" Maggie stood directly under the camera, middle fingers held up.

"Thinking about how fast my dad would've done my mom. He'd already be in the Wendy's drive thru line by now," he said. "What would your parents have done, before they were divorced?"

"I don't think anyone needs data on that. Plenty of men kill their wives without the extra pressure."

The red light stopped flashing.

"Fuck you," Maggie yelled. "Don't want to hear about it, Jen!"

Stan joined her in flipping the camera the bird.

"You have 75 minutes until the door opens and 90 minutes of air for one person remaining," the robotic voice said through the speaker. The light resumed blinking.

"Okay, so," he said. They'd almost waited to have a kid, and as much as he loved Holly, he wished they'd waited longer. Would sitting there, arms entwined, and suffocating together while staring up at the camera be enough to skunk Jenny's data? Make it all a waste?

Maggie came toward him.

He flinched.

"Jesus." She looked at her feet. "Did you think I was going to attack you?"

He trembled. "I didn't think anything."

"Can I hug you?" she asked.

"Of course," he said. She gave great hugs, not afraid to hold on for as long as she felt. He loved that about her.

"Tell me your favorite memory. Of us," she said. She was crying, but addressing the tears would make it worse.

"That's tough," he said.

"I can go first." She looked up at him. "When you met my parents for the first time, and you called my dad Papi, like he was Dominican." She laughed, despite herself.

"But if we call your mom Mummy, it makes sense. They rhyme," he laughed, too, uncontrollably. It ended in a breathless cough.

"You're such a good person. Always giving money to strangers. If Holly ends up like you, it wouldn't be too bad," she said.

"So it's my turn?" he said. Fuck. He hated this. They had so many more memories to make. "When we were flying to Cancun for our honeymoon, and that kid got lost and nobody spoke Spanish at the Denver airport. I didn't even know you spoke Spanish, and you spent an hour translating for him until they could find his parents."

She let him go. "I love you. I want you to kill me." She held the knife against her neck.

"Maggie," he said. He sobbed. He couldn't do this.

"I want you to tell my parents—" her voice cracked. "I want you to tell them that I love them. And I want you to make sure they're a part of Holly's life."

"Of course," he said.

"And have them teach her Malayalam," she said. She closed her eyes.

"I can't," he said as she placed the knife's handle in his hand.

"You have to," she said. She brought the blade to her throat. "Grab the end and pull."

His hand shook on the handle. She smiled at him, wistfully. "Oh Jesus, fuck," he said.

"We have to, for Holly," Maggie said.

He closed his eyes, tears pushing through the crevasses.

"You're going to have to cut hard," she said.

His grandmother had a pool growing up, and they used to dive to the bottom for jars full of coins. He remembered the burn in his lungs on the way back up. Maggie couldn't go like that, gasping for air that wouldn't come. He dropped the knife. "I know another way."

His Boy Scout troop leader had shown him. He had to grab Maggie from behind, one hand on her head and one on her neck and twist. It would be faster and, he hoped, less painful.

"I want you to do it to me, though," he said.

"I can't kill you, Stan."

"Goddamnit. We're running out of time. And we can't leave Holly alone," he said. "What are they going to do with her? If this is how they're experimenting on us, what're they going to do to her?" He remembered an experiment from his Intro to Psych class where researchers found a baby monkey preferred a stuffed animal with no food to a wire mother with a bottle. If Jen tried to do that with Holly, he'd find a way to kill her.

"That's why you need to kill me," she said. She picked up the knife. "Do it. And then you put this out of your mind."

"Look that way."

For once, she didn't ask any questions. She stood up and faced away from him. "Whatever you're going to do, do it now. Before the air runs out."

He came behind her. She'd washed her hair the day before, and her pomegranate shampoo lingered. He put his hands in position, one on her jaw, the other on her neck. "I love you, Maggie."

"I love you, too, Stan," she said, her voice quavering.

The pain in his chest was immense. He looked down and saw the handle of the knife, but not the blade. He felt every inch of the metal inside him. Blood soaked through his white shirt. He gurgled. Shit splattered his shoes. He stumbled onto the table and collapsed.

MAGGIE HUDDLED IN the farthest corner from Stan's still-warm body. She'd seen so many movies where men cradled their dead lovers, but she couldn't bring herself to touch what had once been him. She still felt the knife plunging in. She had wished it had been her until Stan was gone. Then relief had washed over her.

The red light stopped flashing. "The doors will open now."

She stumbled over to the pressure-sealed door, thirsty and hungry. The handwheel spun on its own. The door swung outward with a hiss, leading into a stainless-steel hallway. The air felt so good in her lungs. She pushed a knife out in front of her, ready to do whatever she needed to find Holly.

She heard a cry and ran toward it. She went through another pressure-sealed door, into a room identical to the one they'd been in, except for Holly in a bassinet in the center. Maggie ran to the child, put a hand on her chest to be sure she was breathing.

The door slammed behind. The handwheel cranked shut. A red light in the center of the room stopped flashing. "Thank you for your continued participation, Mrs. Clark. We'll now test the mythical bond of love between parent and child. Welcome to part two of the experiment."

Hard Way

FAKE FIGHTING IN YOUR underwear requires a special level of insanity, especially when you look at the old timers. Mike's head coach, Steve, couldn't lift his arms past his shoulders, and he hadn't hit 40 yet. Lamar, the Tuesday coach, had to have three separate surgeries on his neck and couldn't look left now, and he was just 38. Even Morgan, the Monday night guy, the wunderkind, had a knee that sounded like corrugated sheet metal every time he stepped, and he was only 26.

But Battlin' Bill put the rest of them to shame. He wasn't the craziest because he was big, or even that he hit 50 last year and still looked like a Rob Liefield drawing come to life. Pecs like slabs of beef. Arms thicker than most guys' legs. Legs like a regular person's torso. Not just size, either, but definition. Veins bulging out everywhere. If Battlin' Bill had any body fat, it was in his ear lobes.

Other guys his age retired when the big companies stopped paying the mortgage, but Battlin' Bill worked double the bookings for half the pay. And if he wanted to, he could've stood in the middle of the ring and let guys bounce off him for 20 minutes and call it a night. With how famous his cousin (who would have lawsuitmania running wild on you if he was mentioned by name) was, he could've just done signings and tell-all podcasts. Instead, Battlin' Bill worked hardcore matches.

Bumps on barbed wire, thumbtacks, broken glass. Blading so often his forehead looked like a kielbasa. A Battlin' Bill match was a blood drive.

He looked big on TV, but even bigger in his shockingly normal pickup truck on the way to Home Depot. A pair of readers hung off his nose, and the fabric of his pink button-down looked like it was about to burst. Mike was riding shotgun, and he should've been making small talk, playing it cool. Steve stressed that. When you met your hero, you had to act like they were a regular person. Mike had begged for a match with Battlin' Bill, and Steve had finally agreed.

Apparently, Battlin' Bill liked to be called plain Bill in regular conversation, but Mike was yammering off ideas. "Instead of reversing the powerbomb with a hurricanrana, what if I punch you in the head and then swing around back for a poisonrana?"

Bill kept his eyes on the road, not answering.

"And for the tornado DDT, you could spin me twice," which wouldn't be too hard because one of Bill's arms probably weighed as much as Mike.

Again, no response from Bill.

"Even if we don't do that, would it be okay if I didn't bleed?"

Bill turned down the radio. "Hold up there, kid." He braked for a stoplight across the street from Home Depot. "You seen any of my matches?"

"Yeah," Mike said. Not all of Bill's matches were taped, but Mike had seen maybe half the ones that were. Which would've been close to a thousand since Bill broke into the business in the 80s.

"Then you know, the blood. That's a big part of what I do." Bill sighed. "And who's going to believe that you could knock me off my feet?"

Mike's noodle arms and chicken legs never got bigger no matter how much he lifted. Didn't matter how much or what he ate. Last time he took his shirt off to wrestle a match, some asshole had yelled, "Eat a burrito, pip-squeak." And that was when the crowd was supposed to be cheering him on. It was going to be worse tonight, when people saw him next to Bill.

The light turned green, and Bill put on a blinker and eased the car through the intersection.

"I know, but . . ." Mike didn't want to say it, but Lamar had always told them they had to stand up for themselves. To not let anyone else make them do anything in the ring they didn't want to do. "My mom's going to be there. I don't want to bleed in front of her."

She'd screamed at him after he split his elbow falling through a table off a ladder. *You're going to kill yourself! Why couldn't you have a normal dream?*

"If you say so," Bill said. He drove into the Home Depot parking lot. He drove past some empty spaces in the front to circle behind the building.

"I think the entrance is that way," Mike said, pointing in the direction they came from.

Bill pulled up next to a loading dock. "I know where the entrance is." Bill shifted the truck into park and unbuckled his seat belt and then his pants. He slid his khakis down, getting his ass out. "Do me a favor kid?"

Mike's eyes went wide. "No," he said.

Bill turned to him, readers sliding down his nose. "I got something in the glove box."

Mike didn't want to. But it was Battlin' Bill. And there was the size difference to consider.

The glove box opened to reveal a package of syringes and a vial. Mike breathed a sigh of relief. Bill was taking his pants off so Mike could inject him. It was just steroids.

"You want some, kid? Beef you up real quick."

Mike looked at the vial. Took it out, touched the cold glass. A jar the same size as his mother's vials of insulin. Light glimmered in the clear liquid. He imagined people gasping when he took his shirt off. Shoving his fists down the throats of anyone who dared to laugh.

He swallowed, trying to wet his suddenly dry throat. "How much?"

Bill smiled. Even his cheeks were jacked. "Free tonight. You like it, I'll set you up with more."

Mike had a part-time job shining apples at a grocery store and drove ride shares at night. "Man, I need to know if I can afford it. And like, are there side effects?"

Battlin' Bill, who sold out the Tokyo Dome and Madison Square Garden reached over Mike for a needle. "Two types of wrestlers. The guys who want it and the guys who'll do anything. Take a second and think about it. Which kind are you, Mike?"

Mike didn't answer, but he didn't take out a needle, either.

MIKE PUSHED THE cart at Home Depot as Bill loaded it up with six fluorescent light tubes, 25 feet of barbed wire, and a pair of 50-count bags of steel thumbtacks. They didn't need to buy the cloth bag for Battlin' Bill to put them in. He brought his own.

BACKSTAGE, MIKE huddled on a folding chair, feeling his breath going in and out. He felt the cold of the steel on his bare thighs, heard the sounds of the other wrestlers backstage playing *WCW: Revenge* on an N64, and he catalogued the colors around him. A black curtain. A blue couch. A white first aid kit. He'd wrestled before. It would be okay.

TEXAS EXTREME CHAMPIONSHIP WRESTLING had a ring in the back of All Baseball, so fans, Mike's mom included, had to walk past the batting cages and bullpens to get into the show. Wrestlers had their own entrance in the back, but a couple nights a week during training and most shows, everyone had to move their cars so the delivery truck for the grocery store across the plaza could park for the night.

Once fans got to the door, it was a good space, as long as you could look past the dead roaches. A jury-rigged wall, painted black in the back for the wrestlers to hang out and limber up before their matches. Rows of chairs that Mike showed up two hours early to set up circled the ring in the center of the room.

There was a plywood ramp, and Mike walked down to The Interrupters' "Titleholder." He strutted to the ring, hearing Steve's words—"If you think you're moving too slow, go slower"—and hopped up on the turnbuckle. The crowd went mild. About 20 to 30 middle-aged men, their kids, and his mom sat in the front row on the far side of the ring and golf-clapped. He got his thumbs inside his collar and ripped open his t-shirt, and some asshole laughed as his mom whooped a little too loud.

He hopped off the turnbuckle and went to the opposite corner.

"Introducing first, you know him, you love him, THE—MIIIIIIKE—DROOOOOOPPPP!" the announcer boomed.

Battlin' Bill's music hit: the sound of a jackhammer hitting concrete, followed by a fast electric guitar. This got the kids off their phones and the dads out of their seats. Bill charged through the curtain, light tube in hand.

Mike was still hoping the fluorescent was for show when Bill shattered it over his head. Mike fell into the newly shattered glass. A thousand cuts at once. The bell hadn't even rung yet, and Mike was split open.

Battlin' Bill held up the half-broken tube, "You said you seen my matches."

Over the next 15 minutes, Battlin' Bill dragged Mike to the outside and powerbombed him onto the edge of the ring in front of his mother. Body slammed Mike onto the glass. Poked six little holes into his forehead with a razorblade in the corner, then punched the spot repeatedly to keep the blood flowing.

About halfway through, Mike got the advantage on the outside and knocked Battlin' Bill's head into the ring post. Bill held him there, and said, "Do me, hard way."

There are two types of blood in pro wrestling. The one that comes from razor blades and the one from the "hard way." No blades, no safety.

Mike was happy to oblige, jacking Bill's head into the ring post again and again, CTE be damned. Bill muttered "Wrap your leg in barbed wire. Hit a tiger spin kick."

Bill stumbled into the ring, draping himself over the middle rope.

This was the coolest shit ever.

Bill kicked out at two, and then he took out the black bag with the thumbtacks. The crowd had been eating everything up, with the exception of his mom having a conniption in the front row, but they shifted into another gear as Bill poured out the tacks.

Mike untangled the barbed wire off his leg, which was pouring blood. Bill wasn't much better, a crimson mask dripping onto his massive chest. Bill double-underhooked Mike, the smaller man's legs high into the air, head down, arms trapped. And then Bill jumped up. Landed ass first in the tacks. His thighs padded Mike's eyes, but the tacks stuck into the top of his head. Bill pushed Mike backward and pinned him.

At that point, Mike was done. Even if he'd been booked to win the match, he would've let Bill pick up the W. He stumbled to the back, woozy, as Bill soaked up the cheers.

THE CROWD WAS cycling out, and the trainees were turning off the cameras and stacking chairs in prelude to mopping. Down the hallway, in the back, some of the other wrestlers were playing a WCW game on Steve's childhood N64. Mike's mom made her way past them, toward Mike.

He was hunched over a trash can to catch the blood dripping from his forehead. Steve, in powder-blue latex gloves, searched Mike's scalp for debris. On the way in, the thumbtacks and glass shards hadn't hurt so much because of the adrenaline. Everything stung on the way out.

"What were you thinking?" His mom said. The wrestlers playing the game craned to see around her.

Behind Mike, Battlin' Bill cracked open a tall can of light beer as he waited for his turn under the tweezers.

"Hi, Mom," Mike said. He would rather bump on the thumbtacks again than have this conversation.

"Stay still," Steve tweezed at another tack in Mike's scalp. The skin stretched, and then a gush of blood chased the tack out. Steve dabbed the hole with rubbing alcohol. It stung. The antiseptic smell mixed with the iron of blood.

"Did you hear the crowd, Mom?" Mike asked.

His mom, even in her blue jeans and Mike Dropp t-shirt, didn't fit in backstage at a wrestling show. You could dress her in anything and she'd always be a little uncomfortable, a little out of place, clutching her purse to her chest. "I don't know if you should be doing this."

Steve wiggled a piece of glass. Each move loosened it but practically scraped against Mike's skull. "Ma'am, like I told you when he started, we're professionals. Your son knows how to perform these stunts safely."

"He did a helluva job out there," Bill added, then crushed the now-empty can. "I remember my first bump on thumb-tacks."

"I remember mine, too," Steve said. The piece of glass slipped out of Mike's skull. Steve dropped it into a trash can with a tink.

"Ma'am, your son might be the next star if he can get some weight on him," Bill said.

Mike's mom looked like she was going to burst. "Mike, I just want you to think about it. Is this really what you want?"

BEFORE MIKE LEFT, Bill slipped him a vial of the stuff. "You don't pay for this one. You like it, you ask Steve for my number. You got potential. Do you want it, or will you do anything for it?"

Mike bought some needles on the way home.

MIKE'S SHIFT AT the grocery store started at 6 A.M., a half hour before the truck arrived, so he didn't have time to drop his blood-spotted sheets into the washing machine. Normally, he hated mornings, especially after a show. But that day, he felt more alive than he had in years. Of course, the uncountable cuts and four stitches (from a fed-up nurse at the 24-hour urgent care) all ached. He hadn't slept because of the adrenaline, but there was another feeling, too, like he'd done a three-day-long, full-body workout. Everything was swollen and tight. His uniform shirt barely fit over his chest. This shit was working fast. Too fast.

The cut-fruit girl, Adrean, even commented. "You been working out, Mikey?"

He hated that name but loved a compliment. "You know it." He flexed. A seam on his uniform shirt ripped.

They used a forklift to bring three pallets of fruits and vegetables from the loading bay to the produce cooler. Mike did the work that normally took four hours in two. Even the 50-pound sacks of potatoes felt lighter. He found some needles in the pharmacy section.

At the gym, he injected again.

All of his totals went up around 60 pounds. Mike couldn't stop smiling. He should've done this a long time ago.

He had his first outburst, as he came to think of them, about a week later. His mom made meatloaf for dinner that night. Mike picked out the bigger bits of breading, trying to eat only the meat and onions.

"What are you doing?" she asked.

"Minimizing the carbs," he said.

"Have you thought any more about what we talked about? I know you love to wrestle, but maybe it's not the thing for you." She ate with no compunctions, shoveling down shit.

Anger spiked inside him, uncontrollable. He frisbeed his dinner across the room. The plate shattered. Meatloaf splattered on the wall. Microwaved mixed vegetables stuck below it. A baked potato disappeared behind the fridge. "Goddamnit," was all Mike managed to spit out.

His mom shrank in her chair as Mike knocked his over.

And then his mind came back. He was breathing heavy, an anger burnt through him. "Don't bring it up again."

At practice a week later, his shirt bulged with new sore, cut up, growing muscle.

"Damn," Pedro said. "What have you been eating?"

Mike tried to hold down a grin, but it burst through. "Y'know, a lot of protein. Some mass gainer."

Steve shook his head. "Come to the back after practice. Bill left something for you."

They warmed up with rolls, and when it was Mike's turn, he couldn't scrunch his swollen shoulders small enough to somersault. Something was wrong.

After practice, Steve was hunched over his computer, editing the footage of the show. Later, it would go on to YouTube, one match at a time. They had a handheld cam one of the students held, and a hard cam pointing toward the ring on a platform above the audience.

He held up a finger for Mike to wait as he timed a transition. "Sit," he said.

Mike scraped a chair over the floor. "What's up?"

Steve unlocked the drawer where he kept the cash to pay the wrestlers after each show. "Bill sent more of this for you." It was a glass vial like the one they'd injected from in Bill's truck. "But listen, Mike, I think you should get off of it."

Mike raised his eyebrows. Three months ago, Steve had joked with the Tuesday night coach Lamar about Mike being a bag of bones.

"You're a grown man and I know you're going to make your own decisions, but I think this is a bad one." Steve stared into the vial. "This shit isn't what you think it is. A couple of guys have died—"

Mike shoved Steve, and his chair rolled backward. The anger went 0 to 60, revving toward 100. "You know something, Steve?"

"What?"

Mike snatched the vial. He wanted to punch Steve in his little rat fucker face. The urge to kick a hole in the wall just to break something gnawed at him. He left.

On his way out, Mike yelled, "Get fucked."

Mike hunched over his steering wheel, hyperventilating. Something was squeezing his chest, pushing the ribs inward. He couldn't breathe. Something rippled up his back. The muscles in his brow tightened, bugging his eyes out. He'd told Steve, the only person who'd ever booked him, to "get fucked." Steve, who'd trained him and let him work a match against Battlin' Bill.

What was he doing?

He touched the rubber steering wheel and counted colors in the car. One blue gym bag, one black gear shifter, a brown glove box handle, three white stripes on his wrestling shooters. The anger simmered. The vise loosened around his chest.

"Fuck Steve," he said. He gunned it out of the parking lot.

Two weeks after that, the self-checkout kiosk at CVS was broken, so he had to buy the needles from a girl he vaguely remembered from high school. Madison, her name tag said, but he was pretty sure it was Melissa. She smiled at him.

He wanted to laugh. She would've never smiled at a skinny piece of shit like he'd been before. But now, with his body expanding, here it was.

"Were you in Ms. Barrera's homeroom?" she asked as she scanned the needles.

All of Mike's muscles tensed. "I remember you, too."

"What are you up to now?" she asked.

He handed her his credit card. "I'm a professional wrestler."

"Oh," she said, nodding, eyes wide. "That's the fake kind, right?"

Mike squeezed his hands into fists. People were always asking if it was fake, and it was the wrong fucking word. If it was fake, it wasn't any more so than any other scripted TV show or Cirque du Soleil. Mike pulled up his hair, showing the scar Battlin' Bill left on his forehead. "That look fake to you?"

Madison flinched, knocking into the plastic wall blocking off the cigarettes.

Everything in Mike started tensing again. "Credit card," Mike said and held out his hand.

"What?"

"Give me my fucking credit card so I can leave," he said.

He barely made it to his car. The muscles in his hand spasmed as he tried to unlock the door. The keys clattered on the ground. He dropped the needles. Glass crunched on the pavement. The asphalt scraped his knee as he went down after them. The pressure was in his head, his chest, his arms, his legs, his glutes, everywhere. Something needed to pop.

He didn't realize he was screaming until he felt a hand on his shoulder. "You okay, Mister?"

Some 17-year-old brat was touching Mike. Who the fuck did the kid think he was? He grabbed that little shit's fingers and squeezed until the ligaments and the bones popped.

The kid wailed and fell onto the asphalt.

Mike's ears popped. Blood trickled out, and all at once, the pressure stopped. He fished his car keys off the ground and sped away.

MIKE FOUND AN empty parking lot by the Arkansas River. Light from the streetlamp crept in through the driver-side window as he sifted through the broken glass for an unbroken needle. One had survived.

He didn't know how much he needed to inject to make the shaking stop, so he did all of it.

AT HOME, Mike's mom was waiting by the door. Their apartment was a two bedroom, so it wasn't like she had a whole lot of other places to go, but still it just irked him that she'd sit there while he practiced. Sitting there, hands folded, eyes glued to the table, catatonic.

"I don't want to hear it," he said, when she looked up at him.

She snapped out of whatever fugue she'd been in. Her eyes drooped as she turned to him. "I thought when I left him . . . I thought . . . you wouldn't turn out like him."

Goddamn. He fell onto his scraped knee with a jolt of pain. The hyperventilating was back. And the pressure. His head. It felt like something was growing on the outside of his skull, squeezing the bone. Trying to crush it.

Something rippled from his extremities inward, visibly shaking under his skin, heading for the precious, soft spaces inside him.

"Honey?" his mom asked.

"Mom?" He clenched his jaw. His teeth ground. An incisor cracked, leaking a line of blood. He tasted iron. It hurt so much.

The muscles in his face swelled so big they cracked his orbitals. Then squished his eyes into a mushy mess.

His left humerus went next, snapping from the force of his growing muscles. Something in his tailbone or his pelvis broke with a crack. He dropped to the floor. "Mom," he reached for her with his good arm.

His swelling pecs crushed his ribs. Shards of bones went through his lung. He coughed, choking on the blood. Everything hurt.

His mom grabbed his hand. "What's happening? What's happening to you, baby?" She sobbed.

His myocardium stiffened, squeezing his heart into a bear hug even as the organ fought to keep beating. He drooled blood onto the floor as he tried to talk.

The bicep of his broken arm was the first muscle to pop. Blood geysered. The muscle rolled up his arm, balling in his shoulder. His glutes went next, rushing out into the seat of his pants.

Three more of his teeth snapped under the force of his clenching. His swelling tongue cut against the shards of teeth, one last sting.

And then everything else went. He seized on the ground, each popping muscle sending its own gush of blood, soaking his screaming mother. Then "pop!" went his heart.

Woman in White

"The common fear of ghosts is the fear of being touched by ghosts." —LAFCADIO HEARN

IT STARTED WITH A ZOOM CALL. My toddler wanted to see me, ran around the house yelling Dada for an hour after I left, which was funny because she never yelled Dada when I was home. But you can't get mad at your kids for things like that. Life's too short. The call went as calls with toddlers went. First Beth melted my heart, trying to hug me through Shelley's laptop screen, her hair all done up in pigtails. And then she pointed at the corner of the screen and said, "What's that?"

I looked over my shoulder and everything was as it should've been in the rental. The coat closet door was cracked open because it wouldn't shut all the way. My roller bag leaned against the row of hard cases for my guitars and bass, perpendicular to my amps. Maybe I could've turned on some more lights, but there was nothing to see. Half of raising a toddler was interpreting the weird ways they employed a language they didn't yet grasp.

"Beth, honey, don't touch the screen," Shelley said, voice somewhere in the distance.

But on the computer, about eight feet behind me, I saw her: a tall woman with frizzy hair, impossibly pale and skinny. Hair covered her face, but I could tell she was staring at me. I spun. But she wasn't there. Guitars, amp, roller bag.

I took a timid step toward the closet. Shelley pestered Beth about how far she should be from the screen, but I stopped hearing it. I smelled something strange: an overwhelming rot, like roadkill in August. It got stronger as I moved toward the closet. Instinctively, I didn't touch the spot where I'd seen the woman.

I grabbed the handle, cold metal on my warm hand. Then I swung it open. Hangers banged against each other, dreaming of coats. I didn't bother with one in the Texas fall. On the

ground, a rack waited for shoes. I ran a hand over the top of the shelf. Not even a dust bunny. No space for a person, especially not a tall one, to hide.

I forced out a little laugh. The rotten stench stayed strong. The staticky shiver of eyes buzzed down my back. But I took my seat. "No one's there, sweetie," I said to Beth, even though she hadn't asked.

Behind me, on the camera, the woman stood the tiniest bit closer. "Fuck!" I yelled. Not there physically, but the camera picked her up.

Beth let out a line of gibberish on the other side of the camera. She knew somewhere between fifty and a hundred words, but she'd yet to figure out how to string them together. Pointing and yelling—"Help, milk, doggie!"—generally got her what she wanted before desire boiled into tantrum.

"Mommy, are you there?"

Shelley appeared on camera, hair scrunchied into matching pigtails. Their outfits went together; a pizza missing a slice adorned Shelley's t-shirt and Beth's onesie had the missing piece. "Sorry. Was reading about the war."

If the piss wasn't scared out of me, I might've answered, "Which one?"

"Who is that?" Shelley asked. She leaned down toward the computer.

The strange woman hadn't moved.

"Hello?" I asked. I waved my hand in her direction.

"Why is there a strange woman in your rental house?" Shelley folded her arms.

"I've never seen her before," I said. I couldn't help myself. I checked behind me to see my pile of crap, and then back to the computer where she stood behind it. "Did Beth maybe turn on a filter? Is this a prank you saw on TikTok?"

Shelley clicked on the other end of the computer screen. Beth swatted at her mother's arm, asserting her turn on the computer. "No."

"Shit," I said. I shivered. Static electricity coursed up my arms.

"You're doing that thing. Move to a different room," Shelley said.

I didn't know which thing she meant. It could've been any one of a thousand. I faced the strange woman as I backed into the living room. I searched for a light switch, slapping the wall. She disappeared out of the camera frame.

"I don't see her anymore," I said. I stole a glance at the wall. My hand was groping the wall opposite the switch. Light blasted away the shadows. I spun, looking above the sofas, the armchairs, the TV, trying to find a sign of her.

"Where is she then?" Shelley asked. Beth shouted angrily.

The kitchen by the front door with its little table and my pile of crap stood empty. "I don't know."

"Turn the camera back toward her spot," Shelley said.

I didn't want to, but I did. I couldn't look.

"She's gone," Shelley said. Beth's frustration boiled over into full on screaming.

I checked. No sign of the unsettlingly pale woman. Once, as a kid, I saw a man's open chest hanging in my closet. I stared at it all night, paralyzed by fear. Dad's alarm went off as the sun rose and I finally saw the "man" was actually a white button-down on a hanger, facing out so I'd know to wear it the next morning.

"But you saw her, right? Not a coat hanging on a chair funny?"

"Yeah," Shelley said. "I'm going to give it back to Beth."

My daughter's face replaced my partner's on the screen. "I don't think I should stay," I said.

Shelley's face appeared in front of Beth's, whose shouts doubled in intensity. "Darren, we can't afford to do this twice. You either stay there or you come home. There's no second shot."

I sighed. She was right. This weekend, I was supposed to record an entire album, and win, lose, or draw, this would be it. My last shot at being a professional musician. If it didn't boost the cash I got from playing out three nights a week to 30 grand, I'd hang up the boots, sell most of my gear, and take the job as a paralegal at her dad's law firm. This was the shit-or-get-off-the-pot weekend, and we'd taken out a new credit card to make it happen.

"Okay, I'll stay with the rotten-meat ghost lady," I said. I pictured getting up at eight in the morning and making my way through a soulless office where I'd wear a tie and have to report to HR if I said my favorite word, "fuck." The woman in white couldn't do something worse to me than that.

Look, I know what you're thinking. I've yelled at the screen during the horror movie for people to get out of the haunted house. Just leave the ghost in your dust. But if I left the rental, I'd be leaving my dreams behind with it.

Technically, I didn't have to give up on music if this project didn't work out. But I'd played my first show at 13, and when my 33rd birthday slipped past a month earlier, all I asked for was a laptop with recording capabilities and a weekend alone to make my magnum opus. No party. No gifts. One last hurrah. This album would skyrocket me to where I wanted to be—making a living off this. And if it didn't, no one could knock me. I gave it my all for 20 years.

The rest of my band, the Driller Killers, had peeled off over the last five years. First, Justin took his bass to Nashville so his wife Dani's parents could help with the baby on the way. Then, Al boxed up the drums for law school in Ohio. Michelle held out the longest, but when she got pregnant, she decided to save her voice for the baby. And that left me, the last one standing.

So, I reminded myself that I'd never heard a ghost story where the ghost physically hurt the haunted. I set up my amps, the mic, and the brand-spanking-used laptop in the bathroom, where the acoustics would be best. I hoped that she was somehow confined to the kitchen, where the camera had detected her before.

And for about an hour, I slapped on my noise-canceling headphones and recorded. I wasn't playing my best with the specter and the pressure, but it wasn't shit, either. Sometimes that's all you can ask for. As I lay down a bass track, a video call superseded the Pro Tracks I'd splurged on. I did what any self-respecting musician would and kept playing the track.

The video call wasn't in a program I was familiar with. I didn't have to pick up. One side was me on the chair I dragged in from the kitchen, curtains closed in front of the small window behind me. On the other, a camera looked out into the rental's kitchen. The lights were off, but she was there, looming in front of the roller bag I'd never bothered to move into the bedroom, slightly closer than she'd been before.

I kept thumping out the bass line. Stopping would make the editing that much harder. But I couldn't take my eyes off her. In her stillness, she was magnetic. With the headphones on, I heard something very quiet. As I focused on it, trying to make it out, I missed a note, nuked the track. I hit something out of key, more discordant than it should've been.

When I stopped, her noise got louder. I put the bass down. My heart beat hard, my pulse throbbing against the headphones. I switched the recording input to the video call and started rolling before I turned up the volume. I crept it up, half expecting something to jolt out and blow out my eardrums.

The noise lingered in the lower ranges. As it got louder, I could make out a growl. And then I wondered for the first time who was on the other end, recording her. I'd brought the one laptop, and my phone was off, a brick in my pocket.

A ghost might not be a danger, but another person in the rental house certainly would be. I didn't want to go out there, but if I was going to stay the weekend, I had to confront whatever was going on.

I couldn't find a real weapon, so I held up the chair in front of me as I opened the bathroom door. To my left, the living room and the kitchen stood dark and empty. I slipped back to check my laptop. The call had disconnected.

———

I TEXTED JUSTIN before I called him with the computer. His daughter was in her sixth sleep regression, so the poor bastard was awake, despite 2 A.M. having crept up on us. Black rings circled his eyes as he rocked his daughter. He struggled to enunciate against his sleep deprivation. "What's so important? Why did this have to be a video call?"

"Do you still do that ghost hunting shit?" I asked. In college he'd been obsessed, running around with an EMF reader.

"I don't have time to piss," he said.

"I've got something I want you to listen to," I said. I caught him up and sent him an email.

He bounced Annabelle. Instead of showing signs of sleeping, she seemed to be getting more energetic. He twisted his head so she couldn't swat out his headphones. His forehead cinched. "This is the noise the thing you saw made?"

"Yeah," I said.

"Do you know what evil feels like?"

"No."

"You know that feeling you get when you're shoveling a hole on a hot day and the dirt is caking everywhere on your skin? Imagine that, but underneath your skin. Not like something wants to hurt you, but rage floating in the air like gnats. Do you feel that?"

I checked behind me, the feeling of being watched persisting. Then, I checked the computer screen, seeing only the sofa I sat on. I stole a glance at the spot in the kitchen where I'd seen her. Nothing. "No. It's more like a predator stalking me."

Justin knuckled his eyes. "I'd just go, dude. That growling, it didn't sound like anything that had ever been alive."

"What about a dog?" I asked.

"Maybe," he said. Annabelle pawed a headphone out of his ear. "What's so important about you staying with that thing?"

"This is it. My last chance."

Justin took out his other headphone. "Man, I know that being a rockstar or whatever has always been the dream for you, and no one wants to tell you, but—"

"It used to be your dream, too."

Justin's daughter grabbed at the headphone. "Let me finish. I'm only going to say this once."

"I'm not sure if I want to hear it once."

"We had the dream. We played a couple hundred shows. We sold t-shirts. We had fans. When I think back, I don't think about how we never got rich or had a radio hit. I think about how much fun we had and how much I loved you all. We got further than 95 percent of the people who ever picked up an instrument. Can't you be happy with that?"

"An artist is someone who doesn't quit."

"I don't have time for this," Justin said. He never had time for practice, either. Just excuses. Executive dysfunction.

"I've dedicated my life to this. You think I wanted to man a cash register after college? I did what I had to, to keep the music centered in my life."

"I'm not listening to this again. If you want to stay in the haunted house with your fuc—" he covered his daughter's ears, "—freaking pretentious bullcrap, go right ahead. I didn't quit. I grew up."

Something tall and white appeared on the screen behind him. "What is that?"

"Good luck, I hope the album goes well."

Justin hung up. I thought about calling him back, warning him about her, but I was too fucking mad. If I could go back, I would've saved my friend.

THIS RUMOR FROM the '70s claimed that if you played "Stairway to Heaven" backward, you could hear Robert Plant singing about hell. Satan put him in a secret shed. I wasn't around then, but a middle school teacher told us about it, and in college, Michelle got a copy of the record and we listened. The guitar backward sounded creepier. You could maybe hear the parts about Satan beating them in his shed like people said if you listened extra hard. That dumb rumor sparked my dumber idea: What if I mixed the growling into one of my songs?

I had one called "Shred School," a guitar bash, solo after solo with a roaring melody that I'd been trying to lay down all night. This time, my conscious mind faded into the flow. I put in a layer of growling, then a bass line and a drum track before I put down the rhythm guitar. I ended with the part I wanted to play, the lead. It all came out in a sweaty mess. I came up for air around 4am. I renamed it "Ghost in the System" before the exhaustion my brain had been blocking hit all at once.

I took my laptop to the bedroom, video camera on, making sure that she wasn't in there. Before I passed out, I emailed the song to Al, who would rerecord the drum track on his live kit, and to Shelley, who would lie to me and tell me it's good. But she wouldn't have to lie, because that was the best playing I'd ever done—one of those moments when you ascend to a higher plane as you create.

My alarm buzzed me up at 7, like every other morning. With no kid to feed breakfast, I could've snoozed, but I wanted to get at it. I had two missed calls from Justin and one from Shelley. Texts from both.

I rolled over, and my shoes felt heavy on my feet. I'd slept in them. I grabbed my laptop to check for her. The battery had died during the night. I fumbled for the charger, staring into the nothingness between me and the bedroom's closed door. I searched for an outline, listened for the growling that had been too quiet to hear without digital manipulation. I tapped the power button until it turned on. The camera app popped open. She wasn't in the room.

I sighed and collapsed back onto the bed. I swiped Justin's missed calls and texts into the digital abyss. I clicked on Shelley's to return her call.

"Did you video call me at 5?"

"Good morning. Did you get a chance to listen to the song I sent you?"

"Darren, I'm not fucking around," she said. In the background, Beth blew a raspberry. My brother had taught her to do that when he'd visited a couple of months ago.

"I went to bed at 4. Unless I called you in my sleep . . ."

"You weren't in the video when I picked up," she said.

"What was?" I asked. My heart beat harder.

"Stop that, Beth!" she yelled, face not far enough away from the phone. "The kitchen. That woman."

"Did she say anything? Do anything?"

Shelley shook her head. "Just stared at me. But she was closer than before."

I nodded as I searched for something, anything, that I could say.

"I think you should come home. We can figure out another weekend you can do this. Somewhere else. My dad can float us a little more," she said. She sounded out of breath, maybe crying. Tears came easily to her.

"Last night we couldn't afford it," I said.

"We'll find a way. I'm sorry I've been so down. I've been reading about this war," she said.

"No," I said. And maybe I could have driven the hour home, but we'd chosen this place specifically because it was too far away to just swing by. Would breakfast really have been that big of an imposition? "One more night with a ghost, and then it'll be time for my big break." Manifest it.

"I'm going to do some research. On the property. Who owned it. If anyone died there."

"Thank you for that," I said. It was a waste of time, but fighting with her about it would've been a bigger waste.

Recording Saturday went incredibly well. I laid down track after track, barely breaking to eat. I didn't use the growl sample again, but it echoed in all the songs, like the music had marinated in it. My fingers stung, calluses not thick enough for eight-hour days. I didn't bother with breakfast but sped over to the closest fast-food place, a rundown Burger King, for lunch. My back got stiff from sitting for so long. The toasting roadkill smell hit me on my way in and out of the house, but I gave it a wide berth and didn't bother stopping. I reminded myself that there'd never been a single ghost story where the ghost could physically hurt anyone, and if she could, she was taking her sweet time doing it.

When you make art, you don't know for sure whether anyone else is going to like it. It's a roll of the dice. I'd spent almost a year writing this batch of songs, my magnum opus, and it felt incredible to finally be recording them. And these were some of the best renditions I ever played. Anyone who's ever created knows that it's an incredible high, better than any of the drugs I'd ever taken.

Of course, I still checked for her periodically. I smelled her again when I got back with my Burger King dinner. She even called twice, but this time I just hung up the calls as soon as I answered them. She kept creeping closer to the kitchen table between calls, but it'd be a week and a half before she made it into the bathroom.

The album, at least a rough mix of it, was done around midnight with a day to spare. Maybe I'd go back in Sunday and lay down some extra leads and harmonies.

Or maybe I'd head home. I shouldn't have left Shelley flustered like that, shouldn't have let her calls go to voicemail. I sent her a text letting her know that I was okay but deep in the weeds on this album. I ignored Justin's call, not extending him the same courtesy of a text. I didn't give a good goddamn if he was flustered.

The album was instrumental guitar, more Yngwie J. Malmsteen than Joe Satriani. No one wanted this kind of stuff anymore, but it didn't matter. If I was going to take one last shot, I'd play and let the chips fall where they may.

I hit the sack, this time remembering to plug in the laptop. I slept the dreamless sleep of the dead.

THE NEXT MORNING, I woke up more exhausted than when I'd gone to sleep. I had 13 missed calls from Shelley and six from Justin. The texts filled up my entire phone screen. I sat up and checked the laptop, pointed toward the door. She wasn't there.

I kicked Justin back into the digital abyss again. Shelley picked up immediately.

"Get out of that house now," she said.

"What?" I asked. I still needed to mix the tracks and send them to her and Al.

"She's in your bed," Shelley said.

I spun the laptop around. The roadkill stink invaded my nose before I saw her. Her feet, covered in black soot, were planted six inches from where I'd slept. I scrambled off the bed. I pointed the laptop at her to make sure she didn't come with me. Her hair covered her face, but I could feel the intensity of her glare through it, see it in the set of her shoulders.

"I kept trying to call you, and . . . and the calls kept coming from your laptop. She stood so close to you. She's still not moving, but I don't know. I don't want her to touch you. It's wrong. Do you feel okay?"

Everything hurt like I was hungover, even though I went full sober while I recorded. "No."

"Just come home," Shelley said.

"Okay. I'm packing up and leaving now."

I kept the laptop trained on her until I closed the bedroom door. And then I kept it out in front of me, doing the occasional sweep for her as I gathered up the instruments, amps, pedals, cables, and dirty clothes.

She didn't appear again. As I backed out of the narrow driveway to start the hour-drive home, I thought that this was it.

I try not to be cynical, to not become too obsessed with the marketing of everything, but a thought popped into my head on the road between San Antonio and Austin. I could call the album *Haunted House* or *Notes From the Ghost House*, something like that, and then go on paranormal podcasts and tell this story. How many copies could I move if I capitalized on this?

BETH WAS BEYOND HAPPY to see me. Kids at her age are basically dogs, always wanting to play and being completely overwhelmed by their emotions, living in a constant now. She ran over, screaming, "Daddy, daddy," begging to be picked up.

I scooped her up and kissed Shelley. Beth swatted at us to stop the affection. Dark rings formed under Shelley's eyes, and her shoulders slumped. I couldn't tell if it was because of the woman in white or from spending Saturday alone with the baby.

"How're you?" I asked gently.

"Beth, watch some animals." The kiddo ran to the sofa and climbed up. We'd eschewed cartoons so far in favor of the nature documentaries Shelley clicked on. "Come to the bedroom."

I followed her as she shuffled into our room and closed the door.

"Mama," Beth yelled. Her little feet pattered toward us.

"I did that research. That house is new," she said.

That I had guessed on my own. If not brand new, one of the thousands of houses built for the Californians migrating to Texas in the last decade.

"No one has ever died there, at least not in the news. The land was a farm five years ago. There aren't really records before that, but indigenous people were on this land for centuries before . . ."

"That's a racist trope they made up for *Poltergeist* anyway. The Indian burial ground haunting the white folks," I said. "We're safe now. Whatever was in that house, I left. It's gone. Far away. And I've got an album now. Al's still got to lay down his drum tracks and I need to work out the mixes, but that's it."

"I don't feel like you're listening to me," Shelley said.

Beth pounded on the door. This time she yelled for me, a rarity. Even though, or maybe because, I spent the days with her, she was obsessed with her mother.

"I know it's a racist trope, but what I'm trying to tell you is that there's nothing—"

"I am listening. No reason to believe that anyone died in the house. Justin said that it might have never been alive in the first place," I said. "And I don't feel like you're listening. Have you heard the song I sent you?"

"I've been busy. Researching this, for you. Taking care of your daughter. Have you been reading about the war?"

"Our daughter," I said.

Beth pounded on the door again. This time I opened it and scooped her up.

"Daddy," she said and slapped me in the face.

"Soft touch," I said, though I might as well have been asking her for a pepperoni pizza. I turned to Shelley before I took the baby out. "It's a five-minute song. Would it really take that long to listen to it if you actually wanted to?"

I felt like an asshole as soon as I said it, but I was pissed. No one had asked her to do any research.

I WAS PISSED, hands shaking a little if I'm being totally honest. That happened after every fight. My mom got diarrhea whenever she and my dad had a spat, so physical manifestations of our emotions were some weird quirk of our family genetics. I ditched the kid with Shelley again, too mad to care that they'd be alone together all weekend, and sat at the little desk by our bed that passed as an office. I thought that maybe I could do a little bit of the mixing of pre-official drum tracks, or at least get all of the guitars and keys lined up.

Twenty minutes in, I got a video call from an unknown caller. I clicked the red button to hang up. The ringing persisted. I hammered the icon now, but instead of disconnecting, a video panel invaded my screen.

On the left side, I saw myself, eyes bleary. Instinctively at this point, I checked for her behind me. Which was, of course, illogical. I had left that house. On the right side of the screen, an unmade bed somewhere I'd never seen before. The sheets had an orange-and-blue checkerboard pattern on white cloth. Two pillows were propped against the bed frame on one side, a third lay next to them with a small indent from the head it cushioned every night. In the background, a baby wailed, the sound tremolo-ing.

And then I heard, "I'll change her diaper. Just sit down, pop your titty out."

I recognized the voice but couldn't place it. Then Dani, Justin's wife climbed onto the bed where the pillows were propped up.

She lifted her t-shirt over her head, revealing breasts that had grown since I'd last seen her. Part of me liked it, and the other part wanted to punch myself in the dick for being a creep.

"Did you read the news? A bomb hit a school," Dani said.

I didn't hear Shelley walk into the room behind me because of the noise-canceling headphones. Vaguely, I made out "Beth's down for a nap. Is it okay if we talk?" as she touched my shoulder.

Dani undid the clasp of her maternity bra and let her nipples hang out. I clicked to close the video app, which I hoped I would've done anyway. Of course, it didn't work.

"What the hell are you watching? Is that Dani?"

I pulled the headphones off my ears. "It's not what it looks like," I said. "It's one of those weird ass calls from the woman in white."

Shelley smacked my arm. "Is this what you're doing in the rental house? Wasting my dad's money jerking off to spy-cam videos of our friend?"

I didn't want to touch that hornet's nest. "I don't know what this is. It just came up on the computer. I tried to tell Dani not to take her clothes off."

"I'm calling her right now," she said. I'd made a mistake one night on tour that Shelley had not quite forgiven. She'd done even less forgetting.

"Please don't," I said.

Shelley lowered her phone and asked. "What's that?"

Justin was on the other side of the bed now, and Annabelle was suckling Dani. In the background, there was a rocking chair. A shadowy figure stood tall. And for the first time, she moved. Without stepping, she moved, almost imperceptibly, two inches forward.

"I'm calling them," Shelley said.

"She can't do anything. She hasn't done anything yet," I said, despite the phone in her hand.

"Wouldn't you want to know?" Shelley asked.

On the other end of the screen, Dani's phone vibrated on the nightstand. "Who is it?"

Justin picked up the phone and told her.

"Just ignore it. She can smooth over Darren's problems later," Dani said.

Justin declined the call.

Shelley held the phone away from her face, confused about what had happened. The woman in white's head shifted toward us. Her hand moved forward a centimeter.

I tried Justin's phone, which must've been out of the room. "Call Dani again," I said. "Call again right now."

"What do you think I'm doing?" Shelley said.

On the other end of the screen, the phone buzzed.

"Shelley again," Justin said.

"Put it on mute," she said. "Ow. Tooth." She switched Annabelle to the other breast.

The woman in white's hand edged another two centimeters forward. She was reaching for Dani and the baby.

Justin put Dani's phone on the nightstand on the woman in white's side of the bed.

"Text them," I said. I tried to remind myself that up until this point, she hadn't been able to do anything. But she hadn't moved before either.

Shelley typed furiously.

"She could do so much better than Darren," Dani said.

"He used to be a great guy. Sunken-cost fallacy's got him. He can't stop because he already put in so much. It's arresting Shelley's life, too, working twice as hard to support them both," he said.

I about had a stroke. The two of them judging me. The quitter and the wife who didn't keep him in the game.

Dani's phone buzzed. The woman in white's hand moved an inch this time. Without going over, around, or through it, she blipped to the front of the chair.

"I thought I told you to put it on silent," Dani said. She switched Annabelle to her other breast.

Justin went to the nightstand. The woman in white's hand nearly brushed against his arm as he read off the phone. "Shelley says, 'Call back now.' She says that we're in danger."

The two of them looked around the room. Of course they couldn't see her. Justin's back was to her as he leaned over the nightstand. Her head moved forward this time, close enough that if she breathed, the air would hit Justin's neck.

"He called me about a woman in white last night. And then I got a series of weird, like, robocalls where I just saw her behind me, a little closer every time. Weird prank," he said.

"The spiritual expert," Dani said, rolling her eyes.

"Behind you!" I yelled. Shelley called again.

The phone buzzed in his hand. "It's Shelley again."

"Fine," Dani said, and reached across the bed as far as she could while Annabelle ate.

Justin straightened out into the woman in white. Her head phased into his neck. His eyes went wide. His mouth fell open. He made a strange noise, a mix of a gag and a scream. The phone crashed against the floor. Justin followed after it. Dani yelped, pulling the baby off her breast.

And then the computer screen flickered. Shelley jammed her knuckles against her lip. Something broke inside the machine. The video flashed on and off and made a sound like a piece of paper caught in a fan.

I slapped the screen. "Come back!"

"Pick up!" Shelley stomped her feet.

The video resumed. An empty room stared back at us. The pillows were in disarray from Dani getting up, but there were no other signs of human life.

Shelley dialed the number again. I tried Justin. I think both of us knew that they weren't going to pick up, but what else could we do? I dragged him into this, and something had happened to him, not to me. I hadn't chosen for it to be that way, but people's emotions rarely line up with a logical assessment of the situation.

"Hello. This is Justin. Text me like a normal person, unless you're my mom. You get a pass, Ma."

"Hi. This is Daniella's phone. Please leave a message at the tone."

"Hello. This is Justin. Text me like a normal person, unless you're my mom. You get a pass, Ma."

"Hi. This is Daniella's phone. Please leave a message at the tone."

We called again and again over the next three hours. When our phones' batteries got low, we plugged them into the wall. We texted. We racked our brains for someone we might know in Tennessee, anyone who could check on them. But outside of their wedding, we'd only met Dani's parents once, and they hadn't exchanged phone numbers with the bridal party.

We did everything up to calling the police, and we discussed it, but in the end, what would we say? A magic camera had called us. The video froze when the woman in white touched Justin, so we hadn't actually seen anything bad happening. The only evidence we had was a mountain of missed calls, and what new parents answer every phone call?

Beth snapped us out of it. She screamed in general when she woke. Then for Mama. Then for Dada.

"We'll try again in an hour," Shelley said.

"Yeah," I said. Numbness overtook horror. I'd watched one of my best friends get touched by this thing, and I felt nothing. And then guilt for feeling nothing. Being a person is hard.

BETH WATCHED "Baby Shark" on repeat, the "doot doot doots" not searing through my brain as they normally would. She ate Cheerios from a little pink bowl. We set the laptop on the table, Shelley scanning the room behind us—the kitchen cupboards, a window looking out at our backyard—for signs of the woman. It took her minutes to move feet, but she'd gone from San Antonio to Nashville faster than a plane could've flown.

The numbness broke and a tsunami of guilt swept away the rest of my feelings. A lot of people describe anger as a heat, and I felt that too, but it was followed by these arctic freezes. I searched for something I could do, a way to exercise my anger.

"So you researched the house. New build. You researched the land, no sign of a settlement before the developer built the subdivision," I said.

"Well, I didn't want to say before . . ." Shelley said. She checked for the woman on the screen.

"Say what?" I asked.

"How I got the laptop," she said.

"You did. From the pawn shop," I said. She'd gotten a good deal. I felt bad for whoever dropped it, it was a nice piece of machinery.

Cereal sprinkled the floor as Beth flipped the bowl. "Honey, don't do that," Shelley said and grabbed the broom.

"Wait. What do you mean about the computer?"

Shelley stopped in front of the closet. "I got it from my cousin, Brian."

"The cop?" I said. I'd met the guy two or three times, and he seemed nice enough. I didn't like cops, but I could have a beer and keep him at arm's length at Thanksgiving.

"From the evidence locker," she said.

Potential crimes raced through my mind. It wouldn't be running so smoothly if it'd been used to bludgeon someone to death, so it wasn't that. Best case, my laptop had been used for some white-collar crime in its previous life, insider trading or embezzlement. I didn't want to imagine that it'd been used to shoot or edit porn with sex slaves. Or even worse, a snuff film.

"He didn't say what it was used for. Just that he had this laptop with all of this recording software that he could get for you and they'd wipe the bad stuff."

"What bad stuff?" I asked.

Shelley trembled. "He didn't say."

"Call him," I said.

Shelley's hand shook as she dialed his number and flipped the phone onto speaker. The ringing blasted our ears, always louder than the person actually speaking. Beth slapped the high chair table and said, "Down."

Shelley let the broom clatter on the floor.

That wasn't like her, but I grabbed it, happy to have something to do with my hands. To sweep the cereal into the dustpan, neatly.

"You've reached Officer Brian Hastings. Please leave a message at the beep," Shelley's cousin said. She hung up and sent him a text to call us as soon as possible.

We tried Dani and Justin a few more times but got nothing.

DANI FINALLY CALLED us two hours later. Her voice sounded strained, far off on the phone. "Hi, Darren. Is Shelley there?"

"Hold on," I said and walked over to the nursery. She and Beth were playing with a singing basketball hoop toy. "It's Dani," I said and put the phone on speaker. I brought the laptop, camera open, with me.

"Are you okay?" Shelley asked.

"Yes, the baby and I are fine."

The walls of the room all rushed toward me. I grabbed at the little basketball hoop for balance. I fell over anyway, landing half on it, half off. The height of comedy for Beth, who hadn't yet developed the skill of reading the room.

"What about Justin?" Shelley asked.

Dani paused for a couple of seconds. A loudspeaker beeped in the background. People bustled around her.

"We're at the hospital now," she said.

"Is he okay?" I asked.

Beth grabbed for the phone and yelled, "Hello!"

"Hi, sweetie," Dani said. "I don't know how to say this, but Justin had some kind of event. They don't know what. He was standing there one minute, and then he hit the floor."

Shelley nudged me.

This would be my responsibility, too. "We know. We saw."

Shelley shushed Beth.

I waited for Dani to say something for as long as I could take it. "Something weird is going on. I called Justin about it last night, actually. We got a video call from an unregistered number, and when I answered, it uh, showed your bedroom."

"What?" Dani said.

Shelley motioned for me to keep going.

"Listen, I saw this woman in white. Did Justin tell you about her?" I asked. I made sure she wasn't sneaking up behind us as we talked.

"No," Dani said, words coming out slowly.

"She started stalking me in this rented house. And I left the house. And now we think it's the laptop," I said.

Shelley gestured for me to get on with it.

"We saw her in your room. We called to warn you. Right before Justin collapsed, she opened her mouth and uh. Well she. She—"

"She touched him," Shelley said.

Beth tugged at my sleeve. I brushed her off.

"I don't have time for this," Dani said. She hung up.

I splayed out on Beth's floor. There was so much we didn't know. Was Dani safe? Was Annabelle? And was it my fault if they weren't? There was no way I could've known. But did that matter?

I lifted the laptop over my head, but Shelley grabbed it before I smashed it. "If she's in there and we destroy it—"

"We don't know she's in there and that's the only way we've found that we can see her," Shelley said. She's always been the smarter one out of the two of us.

"I gotta clear my head," I said.

I left the laptop with Shelley, confident that the woman in white couldn't move fast enough to catch me.

OUR SUBDIVISION BOASTED over five miles of hiking trails. Really, they were sidewalks running along the drainage ditches a community like ours needed to avoid getting washed away during tornado season. Dogs barked from their fences, sprinting from one end of the yard to the other as I walked by. I focused on the cool breeze, the crisp autumn aroma. Anything to slow my racing heart.

I moved through a kind of waking slumber until my phone buzzed.

With everything going on with Justin and the laptop, Al slipped my mind until his email arrived.

> *Darren,*
>
> *Loved "Ghost in the System" I'm sending a Google Drive link with the new mixes with my drums replacing the R2D2's. Don't take this badly, but I don't remember you being this good. Like something clicked and you leveled up. Like Goku climbing in 100x normal gravity on his way to fight Frieza.*
>
> *What did you use for the sample? Is that a dog fight?*
>
> *Rock On,*
>
> *Al*

My calm shattered as I sprinted back toward the house. If Al heard her, she could be behind him right now. She could touch him and do whatever the hell she did to Justin to him. Justin was a skinny guy who ran a marathon last year. Al was pre-diabetic and struggling with high blood pressure. Him falling would be a lot worse, not to mention the fact that he lived alone.

Shelley and Beth were still in the nursery, watching "Wheels on the Bus" on repeat, Shelley half zoned out while Beth attempted the dance moves on the screen.

"Laptop," I said, huffing and puffing as I tried to get the word out.

"What?" Shelley said. Beth added, "Dada!"

"Laptop. Al. I used her voice as a sample. She could be with Al," I said. I grabbed my knees and tried to get my breathing under control. I'd never been an athlete. Working out would waste time I could've been practicing.

The small video behind me on the computer popped open as I called Al.

Almost immediately, the call declined. My lungs tightened until my phone chimed with a text message: "I'm at the library. Gotta totes learn all these torts."

"Does anyone answer their fucking phone anymore?" I yelled.

"Fucking," Beth said and giggled.

"Darren, you need to calm down," Shelley said.

I texted Al: "Just call me for ten seconds. Something weird is going on and I need to see you on video."

The typing icon came up. It disappeared, then popped up again. "You've got ten seconds."

My phone rang. Justin. I declined. And then I called Al on the laptop.

Al's mustache resembled the ones worn by lawmen in the candy-coated Hollywood version of the Wild West. He was at a desk with dark brown wooden walls stretching out on either side to block out the person studying next to him. He had three books open, passages highlighted in pink, yellow, and orange.

Behind him, a shelf full of books. I didn't see her any-where. Since she'd hit Justin, she'd disappeared.

"All good?" Al said. His eyes added an essay on exhaustion.

"Yeah," I said. And I really believed it.

CONFIDENT AL WAS SAFE, we ate Costco chicken nuggets, laptop facing us as we watched the latest Netflix show of the week on the TV.

Before bed, we decided to try Dani one more time.

She ignored our call but texted us: "No change. I will update you if necessary."

"She sure is mad," I said.

Shelley smacked my arm. "How would you feel if some-thing happened to me? And then some jackass called you up with a half-baked conspiracy theory?"

"It's fully baked. The toothpick went in and came out dry. We saw the woman in white touch him. What else do you need?"

"Dani didn't see any of that. And you should've recorded it. Wouldn't it be useful to have proof?"

I started and stopped, furious. "You didn't record it either."

"I'm going to bed," she said.

I had a lot more to say, but in seven years of marriage, I had figured out that sometimes it was better to be quiet than to be right.

IN OUR SEVEN YEARS, Shelley'd slept through a Driller Killers show, the source of three years of fights between us. Through a tornado while my parents were visiting, the source of six years of unwarranted criticism from them. In a taxi in Rome. On a city bus in New York City. So it didn't come as a surprise that she slept that night with our laptop on a tray table, camera open but not recording our bed.

I, on the other hand, would wake if Beth farted across the hall. With the light of the laptop, the best I could hope for was a few minutes at a time with my eyes closed. My thoughts stayed on Justin and what she'd done to him.

But most of the night, I watched us, eyes half glazed. I waited for her to walk through the wall. To emerge from the shadows behind Shelley and to put a hand on her shoulder. Or to phase up through the mattress, head undulating out from underneath us.

But she didn't show.

SHELLEY HAD WORK in the morning. I made a cursory attempt to convince her to stay home, but I hadn't seen the woman in white behind her once. She'd gone after me and after Justin.

Maybe she was a sexist, but in that moment, I thought the people that she didn't appear behind were safe.

Beth did not love hanging out in front of the laptop, but I had to know we were safe. My head throbbed, and it intensified every time she screamed—which, if you've ever spent a day with a toddler, you know happens often. Toddlers don't care if you got enough sleep. They want what they want and now.

I wasn't sure I was going to make it. And then the video app on the laptop rang.

Beth and I were in the playpen, two-foot-tall walls built in a six-foot-by-six-foot square filled with random foot-stabbing toys. I rushed across to the laptop, half expecting it to be another one of those calls from no one. But it was Dani.

Hair disheveled, mascara running, Annabelle clutched tight to her.

My gut dropped. Even before she said anything, I knew what happened.

"Justin's gone," she said.

I felt like someone had hit me in the stomach with a sledgehammer. Like I'd been dropped into a vat of wet concrete. All the hopes I had for Beth, to teach her to play guitar, to show her *Star Wars* for the first time, to walk her down the aisle at her wedding if she chose to get married, flashed through my head. Annabelle wouldn't get any of those things. Not from Justin.

"What happened?"

Dani shook her head, fighting for the composure to speak. "Jumped."

"Jesus," I said. I'd called Justin a quitter two days ago. I'd been obsessed with him quitting, like it defined his entire being. The million-dollar question, of course, was did she kill him? I had exposed him to her, and whether she did it directly or not, he was dead.

"I need to go. I'll text you details about the funeral."

"Are you okay?" I asked, but she was gone.

I chucked the pillow I was leaning on out of the playpen. Beth screamed.

I screamed.

I grabbed Beth, squeezed her tight. My little girl. Who was going to hold Annabelle?

SHELLEY SOUNDED FAR away on the phone as I told her. Dis-associating, if I had to guess. Saying the words brought on my first wave of crying. Somehow, saying it out loud brought it to life. Like it wasn't real until I had to tell other people. Grief always worked like that for me.

"Should I come home?"

"No, we're okay here," I said. An obvious lie, but this was FUBAR. Shelley being here might help, but I had something else I wanted to do.

I texted cousin Brian, "Where did the laptop you got me come from?"

I didn't think it would be a big deal, but two minutes later my phone rang. Cousin Brian.

"Darren, how you doing, buddy?" Brian said. I held the phone away from my ear. If he'd heard of indoor voices, he'd rejected the idea entirely.

"Are you recording this?"

"What? No. Why would I be recording this?" I asked.

"You ever hear about this thing called a paper trail? Like, someone does something to help someone else out, a favor, you know. And then they text it to them even though it could get them into trouble," Brian said. "Why did Shelley even tell you? I told her you wouldn't be cool about it."

"I'm sorry. I wasn't thinking. Something weird has been going on with the laptop you—"

"Stop. Do you know that this line isn't tapped?"

"No," I said, feeling stupider with every second of the phone call. But I had to know. To make sure what happened to Justin didn't happen again. It was my fault.

"Okay. So don't say anything else over the phone," he said. He'd be rubbing his temples.

"Can you look into where the Christmas present you got me came from?" I asked.

"Real subtle. I can make an inquiry, but it needs to be done with a little tact. No more text messages. No more talking over the phone," he said.

"Thank you," I said. "Everything going okay for you?" I waited a couple of seconds before I realized that he'd hung up.

AFTER LUNCH I LAY Beth in her crib, still sleeping. I set up the laptop in front of me and flopped onto the couch before I turned on a Steve Vai concert.

The crowd cheered as Steve's band took the stage and played the opening rhythm of "For the Love of God." My laptop rang. I paused the video. Caller unknown.

I didn't want to pick up. I didn't want to see who was on the other end. I pictured Justin, destroyed from jumping, on the other end of the line. I imagined her standing an inch away from me. My chest tightened. I pressed the button.

On the other end of the video call, Shelley was leaning in close to the camera, reading something off a monitor. She let out a machine gun rattle on her keyboard. Her office was smaller than I'd pictured it. Her work wasn't the kind of place where spouses dropped in. Four feet behind her, two white hands and the top of a white chin poked through the wall.

I grabbed my phone, thinking of how Dani and Justin hadn't picked up. I had this recurring anxiety that something would happen to Shelley. That I'd need to cash in her life insurance policy, to sell the house to keep Beth and I alive. And I didn't know how we'd survive after that.

But Shelley answered after one ring. "What's up?"

"You need to get out of your office. Now."

She rolled her chair backward.

"Stop!"

She froze. "Don't move that way. She's behind you. She's still not through the wall. But she's coming."

"Which way?"

"Go to the right, toward the door. Get out of there, come home," I said.

"And what do I tell my boss?"

I looked around, as if a convenient excuse would be sitting next to me on the sofa. "Tell him about Justin. You can't let her touch you," I said.

Shelley moved to the right. The hands and the chin didn't move in the wall. Shelley disappeared off the camera as she went through the door.

"Take a right. She's not following you," I said.

"Okay, coming home now," Shelley said.

We stayed on the phone, listening to the sound of each other breathing until she got in the car. The invisible camera stayed trained on those hands, on that chin, as they poked out of the wall, unmoving.

SHELLEY HAD DONE the legwork: the woman in white was connected to the laptop, not the house. Maybe Brian would be able to clear some of it up when he finished his "inquiry," whatever the hell that meant.

The keypad of our door's lock beeped four times then whirred. Beth perked up. Hands over her head, she toddled to the door as it swung open. Shelley's eyes were red from tears, her hair disheveled. I got my ass over there, too.

She squeezed me tight. "I'm so sorry. Are you okay?"

"No," I said. "But I'd found an illustrated listicle for getting rid of demons." I showed it to her. Our house had three doors: front, back, and a third that led in from the garage. When the laptop revealed the woman in white wasn't there, I spread a line of salt across the thresholds. Shelley followed it up with a line of my grandmother's silver. We didn't have sage, but I boiled milk in a saucepan. Everything we could think of short of calling a priest.

Beth went down for a nap, and Shelley and I sat on the sofa, laptop videoing us both, our eyes red from crying. Our voices hoarse. I grabbed her hand. It had been a while, and even that warmth got me a little hard.

"Do you think it'll work?" Shelley asked.

"I don't know." I didn't, but I didn't need to freak her out.

"I don't either." She touched my cheek, tears glistened over her eyes.

I kissed her.

She backed up. "What are you doing?"

"What do you think I'm doing?"

"It's not the time," she said. She let go of my hand.

"Okay," I said.

"Maybe we should call a priest," she said. We didn't see eye to eye on the organized religion thing.

I sighed. I was an atheist, and Shelley believed in God, but not organized religion. So we coexisted nicely before the problem of the woman in white, maybe a demon, arose. And the first problem we ran into was who in the hell do you call first? They used a Catholic priest in *The Exorcist*, so we called Our Lady of the Sacred Heart across town first.

"You got any better ideas?"

I didn't. Shelley took the lead.

"So you're not a parishioner, you don't have any money, and you want me to come over as soon as possible to help with your self-diagnosed demon?" an older man asked from the other end of the phone.

We tried the Anglicans next and got the same answers.

Even the Baptists didn't want to help us.

That's how we ended up trying the woman from the yellow pages.

Willow Wilbur, "Demon Mediator," had an office down-town, upstairs from a Kinkos. We must've been a sight, Shelley lugging Beth, me cradling the laptop with the camera pointed at us, searching the building for the staircase to the side. The stoned teens behind the desk at Kinkos didn't seem to be aware that there was an upstairs office until we stepped outside and noticed the glass door leading to a staircase. I hit the buzzer before we could change our minds.

Willow waited for us on top of the stairs, long white hair hanging down on her rainbow poncho. "Hello, hello!" she called down, completely incapable of reading the room. Beth twisted away, as if not looking would make the bad thing not happen.

Willow led us to a cramped office, undecorated outside of all sizes of teddy bears and over-stuffed bookcases. One shelf focused on demonology and the rest on mediations and negotiation with titles like *Getting Past No* and *Getting to Yes*.

Willow lit an incense diffuser. "Sage," she said. Then she sat across from us and leaned over her desk. "Have you been keeping up with the news? They 'accidentally' bombed a hospital last night."

"We've been preoccupied by our own problems," I said.

"So, tell me about what's happening."

I sat my laptop across from her, camera constantly vigilant for the woman in white behind us.

Once again, I let Shelley take the lead. And she did a good job, summarizing what had happened with the woman in white. I chimed in where necessary to add a few details.

As she finished, I said, "But she doesn't talk."

Willow half closed the laptop. "Is it okay if I move this? I want to see both of you," she said.

Shelley said yes at the same time I said no.

"The sage should keep us all safe," Willow said with a smile. I had seen that in the demon listicle, so I let her take it away.

Beth squirmed on Shelley's lap as she got more comfortable. She wanted to explore, which in my mind, only ended with one of those shelves giving out and crushing her in an avalanche of new-age books.

"So, what would you say to this demon, to mediate?" I asked.

"Well, I think a lot of people have some misconceptions about the nature of negotiations. Have you heard of fixed-pie thinking?"

We had not. Shelley let Beth down, and she made a slow circle around her mother's chair.

"People think of negotiations in terms of being a fixed pie. Meaning there are eight slices, and your job is to go out there and get as many slices as you can." She punctuated her words with elaborate gestures. "But in reality, the pie is not fixed. And the slices aren't necessarily what you want. For example, I had a client, once, who wanted a $30k raise from the company where she worked. And they were refusing to give it to her. So, I came in, and I asked the important question: what do you need $30,000 for?"

She paused here, looking into my eyes first and then Shelley's. Beth stopped in front of a shelf, head craned up.

"And she said, 'For child care.' And then it was like a light bulb turned on for everyone. It wasn't about the money. And it turns out her company owned a daycare that would take care of the employee's child for pennies on the dollar. She walked out with a respectable raise and childcare, and the company walked out with a happy employee and a couple of dollars in their pocket. Now, I know what you're probably thinking: how does this apply to my demon?"

"Well, yes," I said. Beth took out a gigantic textbook on demonology and dragged it toward us.

"Mommy book," she said.

Shelley took it and thanked her.

Willow smiled and continued. "Let me explain: demons are here because they want something. You might think, they all want suffering, the death and damnation of the human race, but the question we really need to ask is what do they want those things for?"

"But she doesn't talk," I said.

"Actually, it's not that she can't talk. She's certainly vocal. You used her growling as a sample for your song, didn't you?"

I leaned back in my chair. Shelley took the book from Beth, who immediately held out her hands for Shelley to give it back. Shelley complied, and Beth lugged the book back to the shelf where she found it.

"So, what do you want to do?" Shelley asked.

"A seance. At your house. Tonight. Before it gets worse."

For what this seance was going to cost, we should've bought a new laptop.

SHELLEY AND I were playing a game of keep away, throwing a ball back and forth over Beth's head, both of us zombie staring, laptop on a chair between us to watch for the woman in white, when the doorbell rang. We hadn't seen the woman in white since we'd laid down the salt and the silver and boiled the milk, yet the lizard part of my brain thought it might be her. Like this demon would resort to the tactics of a door-to-door-vacuum-cleaner salesperson.

Through the glass of the door, I recognized the shape of the broad shoulders, the purple of the police uniform. Cousin Brian wasn't big on calling or texting ahead.

Grandma's silver scraped against the floor when Shelley opened the door. Beth buried her face in my leg as Brian waved hello. "How's everybody doing? Shelley, didn't I tell you not to tell Darren about the laptop thing? That he might not be cool about it?"

Shelley forced a smile. "Come on in, Brian."

He stepped extra high over the salt. "Gotta be careful I don't knock the rub off. How long are you going to cook the house for?" He kissed Shelley on the cheek and then turned to me. "I haven't seen you since Thanksgiving, buddy." Brian hugged me, which was about as pleasant as a wrestling match the way he squeezed and then slapped me on the back afterward.

Beth abandoned me, running to her mother.

"You'd think she owed me money," Brian said, pointing at her. He laughed at his own joke. Loud.

He gestured for us to sit down and plopped himself down at the head of the table. He pointed at my laptop, eyebrows raised, "What the hell is that?"

"There's a weird ghost woman. She killed my friend Justin. We can only see her with a camera," I said. I'd cried a lot that day. By that point, all my feelings had been scooped out with a melon baller.

"Huh," Brian said, speechless for once.

I shuffled over to the door and fixed the salt and silver barrier.

Shelley sat and hefted Beth up onto her lap. "Did you find anything about the laptop?"

Brian sighed. "Not saying a word until you turn off that video."

I sighed and closed the laptop.

"You sure you want the baby to hear this?" Brian asked.

Beth stared at him. "Hewwo."

"Hi, sweety," Brian said.

"She's not going to understand anyway," I said. Shelley gave me a look like she was going to say something, but I guess the despair floating off me stopped her.

"Okay." Brian folded his hands on the table. "This laptop, it was found." He and Beth had a stare down. "You sure she can't understand?"

"Just don't show her any pictures," I said.

"Okay, well, the previous owner of the laptop was a teenage girl. You might have seen it in the news. Abigail Murakami."

Shelley gasped. It didn't ring any bells for me.

"Well, Abby worked for a neighbor. An older lady, Veronica Dixon. You used to see that kind of thing all the time. High school girl helping a senior citizen. Cooking. Cleaning. Maybe a little laundry and some other odd jobs. But Ms. Dixon had some weird hobbies, lots of old books, that kind of thing. Paid well enough to buy that laptop with all the fancy recording software."

"Oh my God," Shelley said.

"Oh my God is right," Brian said, shaking his head. "We don't know what happened. Some kind of ritual gone wrong. Or maybe it went right."

Brian wrapped his knuckles on the table. Blinked a few times to compose himself. Beth waved at him, but he'd stopped noticing her.

"Abby didn't come home one night, and when her mom looked in Ms. Dixon's window, she saw Abby all torn up. Arms and legs on opposite sides of the room. Head on an altar, eyes ripped out and replaced with her areolas.

"Mom called us. Thankfully, I was off duty that night. The guy who found it, Johnson, he quit the force a week later. And Ms. Dixon? Gone. But Abby had that laptop set up and recording when all of this happened.

"You wouldn't think that Ms. Dixon could do those things if you saw a picture. Her arm was too small to do that, that kind of damage. You know?

"But Johnson saw the video. Cuz Abby was like you. Recording everything," Brian said. He stopped there, wincing from the memories. Something I never wanted to see. I'd avoided seeing the Bud Dwyer video; Two Girls, One Cup;

and most of the other horrible stuff that floated around the internet. I'd skipped the videos of the police killing the black man, though I'd made sure to give money.

"I asked Johnson what he saw, and he said, 'Everything.' I didn't touch it. Johnson was dead a month later," he said. "But I wiped it off the hard drive before I gave it to you. I couldn't do a factory reset without losing the Pro Tracks. But it's gone. And you should be fine. Don't go looking for it and you won't find it."

Shelley put a comforting hand over Brian's.

"Do you think the lady in white is Veronica Dixon?" I asked Shelley, not really caring if Brian understood.

"Who else?" Shelley asked.

"But listen, you say a word of this to anyone, and my ass is grass. You keep this shit buttoned up tight. No friends. Definitely not our parents, Shelley. You tell them and it's all anyone's going to talk about next Christmas."

We agreed, and then we ordered a pizza. The conversation shifted to safe, neutral topics. The weather. How the Cowboys would look good until the second round of the playoffs before they got blown out again this year. I even played Brian one of the new tracks from the album that didn't have her voice on it.

He left about an hour before the mediator arrived.

Willow side-eyed my grandma's silver, smirking, as she stacked it on our kitchen table. She brought her own dust buster to vacuum up the salt around the entryways. Thankfully, Beth slept through it. I would've liked to drop her off somewhere safe for the night, but cousin Brian wasn't exactly someone we trusted alone with a kid.

I expected Willow to change her clothes. I'd imagined a brown robe, maybe black. I didn't imagine a medium wearing a button-down shirt and slacks, but supposedly she was the expert.

Next, she set up orange candles around the table. She refused to put anything under them to catch wax, and I pictured myself scraping the table late into the night after this whole thing blew up in our faces. But Shelley wanted it.

The first argument came when she asked me to close my laptop.

"Then how will we see her?" I asked.

"We don't need to see her. We're going to communicate with this," she said, pulling a red Etch A Sketch from the same worn-leather shoulder bag she'd produced the candles from.

"Look, she touched my friend Justin, and . . ." I choked up a little, unable to say it.

Willow squeezed my shoulder. "I know. But if we're going to talk to her, we need to force her to communicate in a way we can understand."

I opened my mouth to argue, but Shelley cut me off.

"Darren," she said.

So, I did a final sweep of the room. Even with the salt and the silver wards removed, she'd yet to make an appearance. I hoped that she was still on her way from Shelley's work, a 30-minute drive and probably a few days walking.

"When you're ready, turn off the lights and take a seat at the table," Willow said. She sat herself down at the head. She ran a match head against the side of the box. Phosphorus and smoke floated up as she lit the candles.

I sat to her right. Shelley turned off the light. Shadows danced around the room. The chair scraped as she joined us.

"Everyone, hold hands," Willow said.

Shelley's skin felt warm, familiar, a hand I'd held a thousand times before. Willow's felt clammy, over-moisturized.

"We'll start with a greeting, an invitation, to the spirit. It is essential that we do not break the circle we've created here. That circle is our power, our safety. Until we've banished the spirit, we do not break the circle. Do you both understand?"

"Yes," Shelley said.

I nodded.

"I need a verbal response, Darren," she said.

"Yes," I said and fought the urge to rip free from her pedantic hand.

She closed her eyes and bowed her head. I gave Shelley a look, trying to communicate how absurd all of this was, even with what we'd seen. Shelley was not having any of it. She tilted her head toward Willow, like I needed to listen to the old hippie.

Willow's eyes popped open. "Does anyone need to go to the bathroom, to get a drink of water, to do anything before we get started? This could take hours," she said.

"I'm good," I said.

Shelley echoed the sentiment.

Willow bowed her head again. Then she began, "To the spirit that's been following Darren and Shelley. The spirit that hurt Justin. We welcome you into this space. We invite you to use the tools provided to make your presence known. To communicate with us."

I looked around the room, wishing we'd kept the laptop open. I didn't see how her touching one of us would be any less horrible if we invited her in.

We sat like that for a minute or two. Willow's head stayed down. Shelley searched the room too. The Etch A Sketch lay on the table, unmoving.

"To the entity that has latched itself onto Darren and Shelley and Beth, we are here to communicate with you. We want to know what it is that you want, and if we can, we intend to give it to you," she said.

This time, the temperature in the room plummeted. The candle flames all flickered to the left at once. Shelley's grip tightened on my hand. I could feel her heartbeat racing as Willow stayed stone cold.

"We've provided you the means to make yourself heard, Spirit. Tell us who, or what, you are."

The knobs on the Etch A Sketch twisted on their own. A line formed, going down the center before it curved out into a wobbling "J."

"Welcome, J," Willow said. "Are you the spirit that has been following Darren and Shelley?"

The knobs wobbled again. The "N" formed almost exactly over the "J." If we hadn't seen them in sequence, it would've been indecipherable.

"It's Justin," Shelley said.

It hit me like a punch to the gut. I tried to pull away, but Shelley and Willow both held strong.

The spirit drew a "Y."

I wasn't sure when I started crying, but tears were tickling down my cheeks now. "I'm sorry. We're going to help Dani with Annabelle. We're going to do what we can for them."

Willow gave me a quick squeeze. "Justin, you met the spirit that's been haunting Darren and Shelley. Is she there with you?"

Another "N" formed. And then five more, all written one on top of the other, covering the whole Etch A Sketch.

"Justin, we would like to speak with the spirit that hurt you. What is it that she wants?"

The knobs spun faster. More "N's." The glass was nearly completely covered with the black letters.

"Should we shake it?" Shelley asked.

"Do not break the circle. We don't know if the spirit we're talking to is who it says it is," Willow said. "Spirit, tell us what the being latched to Shelley and Darren wants."

The Etch A Sketch didn't shake, yet left to right the screen cleared. Then the letters formed all at once: "She wants them to see."

"See what?" I asked. And was seeing whatever it was that killed him? Mucous overflowed from my nose as I cried.

"Is the woman we're seeing Veronica Dixon?" Shelley asked.

All the candles flickered at once.

"Is that normal?" Shelley asked.

"Has a new spirit entered the room?"

Why had I agreed to turn off my laptop? What had I been thinking? Fear turned Shelley's hand into a vise.

The growl from my recording, loud enough to hear without digital enhancement, came from the corner by the oven. Normally, the digital clock would've lit that space, but impossibly thick shadows blackened the area.

"Is what J said to us true? You want Darren and Shelley to bear witness? What is it that you would like them to see?"

The growls got louder. The Etch A Sketch floated off the table. Over Justin's words, another word formed. "Everything."

"Why is that you want them to see? Is there a crime you want them to solve? A problem they can fix?"

The growling got louder. The impossible shadows closed in around the table. "No." The word was written, but it felt like I could hear it, too. I got a whiff of the roadkill smell I'd noticed in the rental house.

"Why do you want them to see this 'everything'? Will you leave them alone once they bear witness?" Willow asked.

Shelley yelped.

"What was that?" I shouted. I couldn't lose her, too. If that thing touched her, I wouldn't make it. She was the calm in the storm between Beth and me.

"I don't know," Shelley said.

"In this circle, you cannot touch us," Willow said, but it didn't sound like she quite believed it herself.

Beth screamed in the nursery.

Shelley and I broke our hands right away, both of us up, ready to run to the nursery, but Willow held tight. "Reform the circle, now!"

We obeyed.

"Close it out. Close it out. That's my baby," Shelley said.

"Are you Veronica Dixon? Do you want us to watch the video from that laptop?" I asked.

The knobs on the Etch A Sketch circled.

Willow looked at me for confirmation, and I shook my head. "Spirits, we thank you for your time, but you must now return from whence you came."

The light from the oven clock glowed once again.

"Good?" Shelley asked.

Willow released our hands. Shelley knocked her chair down racing to the nursery. I wasn't far behind her.

The Etch A Sketch stopped at the top of the line. It could've been the start of a "Y" or an "N."

"Goddamnit," I said. It had to be true, though. Veronica Dixon wanted us to watch the video. Or hell, maybe the woman in white was Abigail Murakami and she wanted us to watch the video.

Shelley glared at me on her way down the stairs, Beth in her arms.

Our baby looked at me and said, "Milk."

MICHELLE WAS THE only other Driller Killer that stayed in town. I still talked to Justin and Al more. I didn't make an effort with Michelle because it didn't feel like I had to. We'd bump into each other at the grocery store, the brewery, the only bar in town where once upon a time we'd done a couple of shows before they decided we weren't country enough. The shocking part of that was that they'd thought we'd had any country in us to begin with.

She worked from home in IT, and so naturally, we called her.

"Darren?" she asked when she picked up.

"Hey, Michelle. When is the baby due?" I asked. Beth laughed in the background as she held her hand up to the light coming in from the window and attempted to make different shapes with her shadow.

"I don't know if I want to talk to you right now," Michelle said.

I literally scoffed. We'd clashed a lot during the band days, so her being mad about nonsense wasn't a surprise. I wanted more guitar solos. She wanted more big choruses. I liked to pretend that tension was best for the band, pulling toward those two opposite poles would end up with us getting the best of both sounds.

"Between everything that's happening with the war and then Justin dies. You don't come over. You don't call," she said, her voice quivering.

Oh. A painful bubble of emotions sank through my chest. She was absolutely right. "I'm sorry, Michelle. There's been a lot going on."

"Oh. Is one of you 40 weeks pregnant?"

"You're right. I should've checked on you," I said. I imagined trying to explain that the ghost that killed Justin is stalking us, but he'd been the only one of us to believe in that stuff. The rest of us made fun of him. We'd play the *X-Files* theme when he came into practice late, which was almost always the case.

"How are you doing?" she asked, voice softer, apparently satisfied with her pound of flesh.

"Honestly, I'm terrible. But there's a way you can help," I said.

"What is it?" she asked.

I explained about the video and the laptop.

"Okay," she said. "Shouldn't be a problem, but you're going to have to come to me."

WE COULD SMELL the finish line, so we were in the car 15 minutes later, laptop camera pointing behind us in the car. Far off, behind Beth sleeping in her car seat, Shelley pointed at the tiny figure. Veronica, so far away we could barely see her. I shifted into reverse, moving toward her, and then drove in the opposite direction, toward Michelle and the end.

Michelle lived in a cottage, one living room-kitchen combo and a bedroom off to one side. The space was smaller than a trailer, bigger than a shed. A crib stood in one corner, a mobile twisted slowly above it, occasionally chiming its bell.

Michelle looked like a snake that swallowed a watermelon when she struggled out of her chair to greet us.

"Sit, sit," Shelley said.

I hugged Michelle, the two of us lingering after Justin's death. I put the laptop on the table in front of her and checked the video for Veronica.

"Is it okay if I minimize whatever this is?" Michelle asked.

"Yes," Shelley said, before I could say no. "This is almost over," she said to me.

It took Michelle about 20 seconds to open the computer's trash bin. "It's still here," she said, and double clicked the video.

I shoved past her to close the video that popped open. "We're going to watch it at home," I said.

"Okay, weirdo," Michelle said. "All you needed to do was check if he emptied the trash. You didn't need to come all the way over here."

"Well, it's good to see you," Shelley said.

We all sat down. Beth snored in her car seat as the conversation shifted into Michelle's kid, a girl she'd name Bruno for reasons that I didn't understand even after she'd explained them. I reopened the video browser, but Shelley was across from me, so the camera couldn't capture us both.

I tried to nonchalantly sweep across the room when Michelle asked, "What's going on there, bud?"

I snapped the laptop back toward me. Behind me, through Michelle's open bedroom door, something white caught my eye. I held up a finger to shush her. "Shelley," I said.

Shelley ran to my side by the computer.

"Someone want to tell me what's going on?" Michelle asked.

Shelley walked toward the bedroom.

"What are you doing?" I shouted. Beth woke, screaming again.

Shelley pushed the door the rest of the way open. "Curtains," she said.

I let out a breath I hadn't known I'd been holding. "Michelle, we gotta go," I said.

———

AL EMAILED ME the tracks, all of them, done. But I didn't bother opening the email. Bigger fish wanted to fry me.

IT DIDN'T TAKE long to get Beth back to sleep in her crib. I opened the laptop for what I hoped would be the last time. Shelley came back down the stairs, looking every bit as exhausted as I felt.

"Should I make some popcorn?" she asked.

I laughed, an empty, hollow sound.

I might have said it before, but it bears repeating: I don't watch videos of people dying. Add in that Brian, who'd presumably seen some gristly car wrecks and the like while on duty, looked green at the gills just talking about it, this was the last thing in the world I wanted to do.

But we had to.

Cold sweat from my armpit rolled down my side. I couldn't catch my breath. Shelley sat next to me. We were fairly certain that Veronica couldn't get past the salt-and-silver barrier, but it didn't stop me from checking for what I hoped would be the last time.

I clicked play on the video.

It started with Abby, a teenage girl, practicing a TikTok dance. Her eyes were so bright, full of life. The dread of knowing what was coming made me nauseous.

And then Veronica entered the frame. Her hair was gray and up. I exchanged a glance with Shelley.

"Maybe her spirit manifests differently, like her younger self had that black hair," Shelley said.

It didn't sit right.

On the screen, Veronica said, "It's time."

Abby frowned but grabbed the laptop and followed Veronica into another room. Bookshelves lined the walls with leather-bound volumes. Lit candles and a line of white powder circled one particular book in the center of the room.

"Kneel in front of the book," Veronica said.

"Are you sure?" Abby asked. She set the laptop down, camera framing the candles.

"Do you want the money or not?" Veronica snapped.

Abby sighed. I wondered what it was she wanted the money for. She knelt in the circle. "Do you really think it's going to work this time?"

Off screen, Veronica snarled something too low for the camera to pick up.

Abby high stepped over the salt and knelt in the center. She twirled the book's ribbon around her finger.

"Now read," Veronica said.

Abby started.

"Is that Latin?" Shelley asked.

"Fucked if I know," I said.

Abby kept reading. Maybe if I went back and watched the video again, I could write out something that approximated the sounds. But I will never go near that video again.

On the screen, Veronica chanted in harmony with Abby.

A diminished fifth above her, to be exact. The discordance hurt my ears.

The candles blew in an impossible wind. Abby pinned the page she was reading with a finger and kept going.

Then, a noise like thunder. So loud that the microphone maxed out, turning the sound into a garbled, eardrum-punching mess. Whatever it was hit hard enough to send the laptop taking the video tumbling onto its side in time for us to watch the salt hop from the impact.

"Should I keep going?" Abby asked.

"We can't stop now," Veronica answered.

At this point, we could only see Abby from the calf down and the candles surrounding her. The kid had spunk. She kept reading. A few more seconds and Veronica brought back that horrible harmony, the flat fifth, one of the worst sounds in music.

Something hammered again. The laptop bounced. The salt hopped again, breaking the circle. But we were the only ones that could see it.

"I think we should stop," Abby said.

"No. No, no, no. Once we've begun, we need to see it through. Can't you see? It's working!" Veronica's long dress brushed past the laptop. "Think about what you'll do with all the world's secrets unlocked. The power we'll wield."

Veronica started the chanting this time, and Abby soon joined her.

This time, they stopped on their own. No crash. Veronica lifted the laptop. Abby stood in the center of the circle, brushing salt from her knees. "Did it work?"

The laptop crashed onto the floor. Veronica choked on something. The camera only picked up the keyboard and the hardwood floor, so we heard what happened next.

"Are you okay?" Abby asked. Her bare feet slapped over to Veronica, who couldn't stop choking. "Ms. Dixon?"

Something slammed against the floor, writhed against it. Something cracked, like a stick over a knee.

"Oh fuck," Abby said. Her footsteps backed away.

A footstep so heavy that the laptop bounced.

Abby's lighter footfalls broke into a run, but a door slammed. A doorknob jiggled. Abby screamed, the kind of guttural howl that would leave her throat raw for days. There was a loud snap, like ice breaking on a frozen lake. And then a wet squelch. Something crashed onto the floor by the laptop. The screaming got louder, mixed with tears now.

"Stop," Abby said.

Blood flowed beneath the camera. Another snap, a gunshot in a quiet forest, sounded. Followed by a horrible ripping. By the third, Abby had stopped screaming. It kept going like that, but it was like my brain turned off. I was watching me and Shelley watch the video from above.

Finally, Veronica picked up the laptop. The blood over the camera shaded the world red. Her hair was disheveled, face smeared with crimson. Pieces of Abby were scattered across the room behind her. She cried.

"It worked," she said.

I'm not sure where she got the knife, but she dragged it across her own throat in one quick motion.

For the last time, the laptop crashed onto the floor. And finally, the video ended.

MY HANDS WOULDN'T stop shaking. Shelley pushed back from the table. She waited for a second, maybe searching for her calm, before she threw up in the sink. I tottered over to the sofa and turned on the TV. I scrolled through the shows on streaming until I found the stupidest sitcom I could. Shelley took a seat next to me, and we watched it until 2am, work and baby the next day be damned.

"Is it over?" Shelley asked me.

"It must be."

"Where did her body go? Brian said there was one."

Some questions have no answers.

WE WAITED A DAY before we vacuumed up the salt and cleared the silver for the last time.

I didn't use the laptop in the TSA security line on the way to Justin's funeral. I did check at our gate, but I felt safe going onto the plane. Stressed as hell trying to keep Beth from singing ABC's loud enough to drive the other passengers insane. I started thinking about what it was like flying pre-kid, and how mad I used to get when I got stuck in a seat next to a kid.

I checked again when we got to our seats, but once Beth passed out on Shelley's lap, I had the most peaceful sleep I'd had in months.

And then it was travel as usual. Dragging Beth's car seat off the jetway. A long line at the rental car station. A hotel clerk who wanted to be anywhere else, and I didn't blame them. We ironed our black clothes and then went to the wake.

Dani stood in front of a closed casket, Annabelle nowhere to be seen. I looked down at Beth, dressed in black, trying to break out of Shelley's handhold to explore the rows of chairs set up facing the coffin. We were in the back of the line. I smiled at the people I knew. Justin's brother, who'd come to a lot of our shows. His parents, who'd seen us play on a tour in Cleveland. Some of his cousins who'd come to party with us at college. A few other friends that we hadn't seen since Justin and Dani's wedding. If not for the death, this thing might've been fun.

"Do you know if Al's coming? I owe him an email," I said to Shelley.

"No idea," Shelley said. "Honey, stay with Mama."

The line moved slowly. All at once, people started checking their phones.

"What happened?" I asked even as I reached for mine in my pocket.

"Al," Shelley said, quicker on the draw than I was. "It's on Facebook. He jumped out of the plane on his way here."

"What?" The video was everywhere online.

Al knocked down a flight attendant. Then he looked right into the camera. "I saw it. Everything," he said. Another flight attendant tried to wrangle him, but Al was a bear of a man. And then the door burst open. Everyone screamed. Al disappeared into the clouds before the video ended.

My knees buckled. I grabbed one of the chairs, and it fell down with me. I saw Dani first when I looked up, the widow in black, jostled from her spot at the front of the room. Beth wailed. The funeral director, a tall man with a sepulchral face, helped me up. He led me to an isolated room in the back as everyone stared.

"This happens more than you think," he said. "Were you close with the deceased?"

I nodded, not knowing if he meant Justin or Al. But it didn't matter. The answer wouldn't change. The Driller Killers had gone from touring Texas to Kansas two years ago to only having two living members.

The laptop was at the hotel. I couldn't check for the woman in white. Shelley and a now-calm Beth came in. The baby reached for me, a rarity, and I took her.

"Daddy's okay," I said. I scorned the idealist self who'd promised that he wouldn't lie to his child.

"Let me get you a glass of water," the funeral director said. He shambled out the door, leaving us alone.

"If she got Al, we might still be on the list," I said.

"The video's tattooed onto my brain. What else could she want?"

"Maybe we need to show it to someone else," I said. It had been in the room with Dani, but I couldn't imagine broaching that conversation with her. Not here. Not now. I wanted to throw up, but I swallowed down the feeling.

Along with the video of Al, the sounds of Abby being torn apart played in my head.

Then I smelled rotten meat. I whipped round in its direction.

"What is it?" Shelley asked.

"Do you smell that?" I said. I got up, facing the stink. I put myself between where I thought she was and Shelley.

"No." Shelley wrapped a finger around my belt and led me out of the room.

"It's gone now. We need to go."

"Let's go. Dani will understand," Shelley said.

I didn't think she would, but I didn't much care, either.

A STIFF WIND whipped across the parking lot. I kept sniffing, searching for her stench. I got the falling leaves, the cool autumn air, but nothing rotten. Beth sucked one thumb while running the other through her hair. She'd fall asleep soon. Shelley ran ahead for the rental car, one of those ugly vehicles that looked like a square with wheels.

I did another smell check as I loaded Beth into the travel car seat. She needed a diaper change, and the pine air freshener was doing its job. The engine turned over, and a local butt rock station came on. I clicked on my seatbelt in the passenger seat and brought up directions to our hotel.

I kept sniffing. The only contingency plan I could think of if she appeared in the car would be to bail out. I'd seen a thousand movies where someone jumped out of a car and rolled away the extra momentum, but I hadn't been in a gymnastics class in 20 years, and then I had to wait outside with my mother as my sister practiced. And even if I survived bouncing down the road, she would still be with Shelley and Beth, doing whatever it was she did to them.

I turned off the radio. "I love you," I said.

Shelley squeezed my hand. "I love you, too, Darren."

I twisted back toward Beth. "I love you, sweetie."

Her drooping eyelids perked up enough to give me a dirty look for interrupting her attempted sleep.

"We're going to be okay," Shelley said.

But she didn't know that. The same lie I'd told Beth. The same lie so many of us tell ourselves every day, when in reality, we don't know if we'll be okay. How many people assume that it'll be a day like any other before they're killed in a car crash? Before their hearts burst? Before any of the thousand accidents we all avoid daily hits?

Shelley drove up to a Waffle House.

"What are we doing here?"

"Go in. Get some salt," she said.

I was glad I married someone smarter than me, terrified to walk into the restaurant without being able to see her.

A host greeted me. The smell of the perpetually frying hash browns hit me first. My mouth watered a little. I'd been so caught up, I hadn't felt the pangs of hunger in my stomach. They could wait. I walked to the closest table and grabbed a saltshaker. Then another from the next table.

A man yelled from the table. The host tried to grab me. I ran past them both.

We pulled into the hotel parking lot, only the sound of the humming engine filling the empty air. I got out and did another smell check before I grabbed the car seat. Beth had finally capitulated to the nap, and I carried her as level as I could, quiet as a mouse while Shelley grabbed the salt. Our room was on the third floor.

The elevator doors dinged open. There was a faint scent, like someone had taken a piss in there six months ago. The stairs were another 20 yards down the hall. I couldn't do three flights with Beth in the car seat and keep it level enough for her to stay asleep. So, I got in, and I pictured the elevator stopping. The woman in white floating out of the wall while we were trapped. I saw her touching me.

The machine jerked to a stop and the doors rolled open. Another bullet dodged. I ran to the room and fumbled for my room key. The laptop was still in my carry-on. I flipped it open and alternated machine gun hits on the power button and the enter key.

Shelley grabbed the charger and searched the wall for an outlet.

The smell came back, in the far corner of the room. "Now, honey," I said.

Shelley jammed it into the wall and tossed me the DC adapter. I plugged it in. The first in the series of startup logos popped onto the screen.

I bowed my head. "Oh, thank God."

Something reeked in the far corner of the room, but it seemed to be staying put. Finally, the computer finished booting. My nose was wrong. Or she was still completely in the wall.

Shelley and I pulled the bed away from the wall and traced the perimeter of the room with the salt. It didn't help with the smell, so I did another check with the laptop before I flopped down. Shelley lay down beside me. Beth snored quietly from her car seat on the floor.

"You know we're going to have to call Dani to apologize," Shelley said.

I groaned. She was right, of course, but I could feel the awkwardness already. A sob came out of nowhere. First Justin, now Al. To lose two friends in three days.

Shelley pulled my head onto her. She ran her fingers through my hair. "Let it out."

And then she stopped, rolled out of bed. "Darren, move," she said.

I sat up in bed in time to see her on the laptop screen, the woman in white, coming out of the mattress.

THERE WAS NO TIME. She'd outsmarted us. The salt couldn't seal out something already inside. Her hand touched the back of my head. Her fingers icy tendrils. The force of her touch knocked me upward. It was impossible to resist, but also excruciatingly slow, a centimeter a minute. At first, I couldn't see anything, like my face was too close to a TV screen to make out the image. Shelley's screams took on a muted quality, as though an ocean had formed between us. The noise froze, stretching for eternity.

I kept going, that centimeter a minute until I turned back and looked down on my own body from the outside. Behind me the woman floated out through the bed, moving at a regular speed while I flopped through concrete. Her black hair still covered her face.

And then, ever so slowly, she reached up and parted her hair. There was an abyss where her face should've been, the blackest black I've ever seen. The void swirled into infinity.

The growling and the rotten meat smell came from the black hole in her face.

It started spinning, like a blender. I tried to force my arms and legs to move. To swim away from that gaping maw. But my astral form was paralyzed. Impossibly slow, it sucked me in. First one foot disappeared into it. Then up to a knee. Then the other leg. It wasn't wide enough to fit me, but I shrunk away. The blackness overtook my waist and my chest. My immobilized arms went next. And then she was up to my neck.

I couldn't speak, but I thought that we had done what she asked. That we'd watched the video.

And then I went into the blackness.

Inside, she showed me exactly what she'd promised: everything. Every ounce of pain and suffering in the world. I saw it all at once. The people being bombed in the hundreds of conflicts around the globe. The people starving. The families left behind after their loved ones' car accidents and heart attacks. Dani explaining to Annabelle that Daddy wouldn't be back. Al's parents as they watched the repeated news coverage of their son's suicide. And I didn't just see it all. I felt it. The weight of all that pain falling on my shoulders.

This was her everything.

And worse: she showed me what I could do about it. I couldn't stop a war or feed the starving. I could maybe comfort the few mourning I knew, but there were billions worldwide suffering. All I could do was record my little songs that a couple of friends and family would listen to. What's a guitar solo to someone whose leg got burnt off?

I don't know how long I spent in there, plugged into the nervous system of humanity. It could've been a minute or a thousand years. Either way, it destroyed me.

I don't remember returning to my body. But when I did, I pushed past Shelley and jumped out the window. I couldn't exist while I felt all that pain. From the third floor, I ended up with 13 broken bones. When I'm healed enough, they'll release me to a psychiatric-care facility, where I'll try to trick them into thinking I'm okay enough to let me out. Because I can't exist like this. No one could.

Shorn on the
Fourth of July

I T WAS SEEING HER BROTHER, still 18 but with a newfound confidence and grabbing a beer from the cooler, that set her off at the Fourth of July Party on July Third. It was a snoozefest, and her mother's boss Jed was going on about some new machine he'd built that was going to revolutionize lawn care, and George was taking a beer from the cooler.

Kris was standing on the lawn, watching through the light-blue railings of the deck. "Mom!"

Instead of stepping in to stop George, her mother shushed her.

"This is going to revolutionize the way people cut their lawns," Jed said on the deck. He swung his glass. The brown liquor sloshed right to the edge of his cup but didn't spill over.

So that was how it was going to be. Kris walked up the steps, wove her way through the tech bros and bro-ettes, and found the cooler. She plunged her hand into the icy water.

Her mom, displaying some serious ninja skills, grabbed her arm. "This is my boss' party, Kristina. What do you think you're doing?"

Kris' hand was freezing. The hard glass of a bottle made her fingers tingle. "But George," she said, and pointed with her free hand.

George was on the opposite end of the deck, listening to Jed with the tech bros. He looked like one of them with his button-down blue shirt hanging open over his cargo shorts and Tevas. He'd been away at college for nine months, and suddenly he got a whole new set of rules.

Kris shivered. Her hand was going to come out of the cooler encased in a block of ice.

"He's an adult now," her mother said. "Even if I don't agree with his choices, he gets to make them."

"How come he was allowed to get his permit when he was 15?" Kris asked.

Her mother got a thousand-mile stare.

Kris dropped the beer, for now.

She went into the garage and grabbed her bike first thing the next day.

It was an embarrassingly neon green, the color a fifth grader would pick. She'd asked for a new one for her birthday the last two years, but there was nothing functionally wrong with the one she had.

She'd taken a pair of scissors and clipped the tassels from the once-white handlebars. If her mother weren't so worried about Kris inhaling the fumes, she would spray paint the bike herself and solve the problem. If Dad were still here, he would've let her.

"Where are you going?" her mom asked. She was standing in the doorway, hands on her hips.

"Out," Kris answered. She was going to get that beer.

"I love you, and I hope that we can watch the fireworks together."

Kris didn't answer.

SHE BUNNY-HOPPED the curb and rode her bike onto Jed's lawn. His house was huge. Like massive, but it was designed to look like a single-story ranch in the front. Her mother had told her Jed didn't want people to know how rich he was. There were trees on the sides to keep neighbors from noticing how the house stretched a soccer field and a half.

Finally, she turned the corner and saw the deck. Like she'd expected: the cooler was still there from the Fourth of July Party on July Third.

"Are you embarrassed now, Mom?" she asked.

She dropped her bike by the steps.

There was a buzzing on the other side of the house. Someone mowing the lawn?

She hopped all three steps in a single bound and beelined to the cooler. Today, the water around the beer was warm. She grabbed a Budweiser and propped her phone up on the railing above the cooler. The angle was perfect. She hit record and stepped back from the camera.

"Hey everyone," she said. "This is your girl, Kris. Yesterday my mom said, 'No beer for you.'" She lowered her voice and wagged her finger at the phone. "But newsflash, Mom, I am ten times more mature than George has ever been or will ever be."

She grabbed the cap and twisted. It didn't budge. The metal grated her fingers. "Ah!"

It wasn't a twist-off.

The buzzing got louder as the machine came into the backyard. To her relief, there wasn't a person pushing it. It was a circle, a little bigger than a manhole cover. She couldn't see the blades from above, but she saw the grass shorter in its wake.

So, this is what Jed had been bragging about yesterday. His shock of white hair sticking up, ungelled and uncombed, as he waved his drink around. The Lawn-Ba.

She found a bottle opener on the glass-top table, thankfully shaded by an umbrella. Perfect. She restarted the recording, in hopes that her mic would suppress Lawn-Ba's racket.

"Hey party people," she said. "Yesterday my mom told me I couldn't have a beer and George could." She cracked open the beer and took a swig.

Oh, God. It was awful. Like cat piss. But for the sake of the video, she said, "Ahh."

"Mom, if you're watching, I'm more mature than George has ever been or ever will be." She drank more beer. It was worse the second time. As if bitterness and bile had a baby. She smiled like it was the best thing she had ever tasted.

She went to take the phone down as Lawn-Ba bumped into the deck. The phone flipped in the air. She lunged. It splashed into the cooler. Lukewarm drops of water sprinkled her face.

"No, no, no, no," she said.

She could hear her mother already. "I guess you weren't ready for that responsibility." "A phone is a tool, not a toy." Or "We don't have the money for another."

She could hear George, who would be worse with his kindness. "Don't worry, baby sis. Everybody makes mistakes." He was only three years older than her.

The kids at school. They would find out. They were like sharks, smelling shame from a mile away.

"Eat shit, Lawn-Ba," she yelled at the robot, which was still backing up and going forward into the deck.

The machine paused, as though it had heard her. There was a mess of buttons on the top of it. It was supposed to be white, to look like an Apple product Jed had said, but the grass had stained it green. It was acting as though it had heard her, which was impossible.

That didn't stop it from strafing right. It was alarmingly fast. Much faster than she could run. It moved like a predator attacking. It kept going until it hit Kris' bike.

"Oh, no," she said.

The metal blade tore through her back tire with a thunk. Pieces of hot rubber sprayed out. One caught Kris in the fore-head. It was warm. As she peeled it off, she saw Lawn-Ba wasn't stopping and dove under the table.

The machine gnarled the spokes. They whirred through the air. Three poked through the cooler's lid. Kris dragged it backward to get under the glass-top table.

Lawn-Ba hit the bike's frame next. Metal screeched against metal. Aluminum flew. A shard of shrapnel hit the side of the cooler. Water burst onto the deck. Kris' beer exploded. Metal pelted the side of the house.

"Security breach detected," a mechanical voice said. Steel shutters crashed down behind the windows and the deck door. It did nothing to protect the glass.

Kris kept her head down, listening to the symphony of destruction around her. The wood railing chipped. A section of it fell onto the lawn.

The chain of her bike soared over her. It hit the sun umbrella above the table and tangled around it like a bola. She waited for the umbrella to fall, holding her breath.

As she exhaled, the top half of the umbrella listed forward as though it had felt her relief. It crashed down onto the glass tabletop. Cracks spiderwebbed through it. She pulled herself into as tight of a ball as she could.

The first piece of the tabletop that fell cut her pinky.

She couldn't tell where the other shards hit. It was a rainstorm of pain. The umbrella itself fell on her last.

She didn't know how long she stayed there before the sounds of her bike's destruction stopped.

She shrugged the umbrella off and stood within the table's frame. Neon-green pieces of bike were embedded in the siding. They'd shattered Jed's windows and scratched the steel shutters behind them. A chunk of handlebar had miraculously landed upright on the still-standing half of the umbrella.

The Lawn-Ba was trying to get up the steps now. It went forward and reversed, bumping the bottom step. It backed up and bumped it again.

SHE CHECKED THE gashes on her arms. She could feel the cuts on every part of her back that her tank top didn't cover. She'd needed stitches under her chin after an ice-skating accident when she was younger, and none of her cuts now were as deep as that. At least, she didn't think so. They all stung.

She cracked open one of the surviving beers and dumped it over the cuts to clean them. The stinging got worse all at once, like butter sizzling on a skillet. She wanted to writhe on the ground, but the deck was sparkling with glass.

Lawn-Ba buzzed and bumped. The sun was getting higher, and the temperature was getting hotter. Her phone was dead. Jed's house was shuttered. It was at least a soccer field's distance to the front door. Even if she weren't cut, she'd seen how fast Lawn-Ba had turned toward her bike. There was no outrunning the machine.

She stopped and took an inventory of what was around her. She had the deck chairs. The pieces of metal. Both halves of the sun umbrella. She needed a plan.

Her mother would be broken if she lost Kris. After Dad's accident and George moving out. Half a bottle deep in Costco sangria, Mom told her how much she needed to have someone in the house. George reiterated how much Mom needed her. Nevermind that Kris was 15, that she was supposed to be the one who needed.

Lawn-Ba buzzed and bumped some more as a plan formulated in Kris' mind. Lawn-Ba had shot bike everywhere, but it had taken time.

First, she threw all the chairs but one over the railing, creating an obstacle course for the machine. She tossed the last one in front of Lawn-Ba when the machine reared back.

She sprinted to the far side of the deck and grabbed the umbrella. She waited to hear the blade against the chair before she jumped the railing.

The trees were penned in by a fence. She touched it with the umbrella. "Security breach detected," the same voice that had shuttered the house said. The fence let out a blue shock.

She ran another ten yards toward the front of the house before the noise of the first chair's destruction ceased.

Within five yards, she realized that Lawn-Ba wasn't going after the other chairs.

When she'd run about 20 yards, Lawn-Ba careened around the corner.

"No," she said.

The machine shot toward her.

A branch low enough that she could grab was five yards in front of her. She reached deep and ran hard. Lawn-Ba's blades got louder.

It couldn't have been more than six feet away from her when she got to the tree. She dropped the umbrella between her and Lawn-Ba.

The machine dodged around it. She grabbed the branch. The plastic casing over Lawn-Ba's blades hit her foot as she swung upward.

She hugged the branch. The tree didn't shake with the force of Lawn-Ba's strikes. The bark irritated the cuts on her arm as she wriggled up, but she powered through the pain.

When she'd wrapped her legs around the branch, she looked at Lawn-Ba. The machine had stopped directly below her.

"Why are you doing this?" she asked. "What do you want?"

Of course, Lawn-Ba couldn't answer. It stayed there, blades whirring. With it underneath her, she could see the buttons better now. There was a giant power button with a keypad underneath it.

She spun herself around on the branch so she was facing right-side up. Her blood and sweat coated the tree.

Lawn-Ba stayed underneath her, blades cutting menacingly. They'd torn through the frame of her bike. What would they do to her?

She wondered what her mother was doing. Cutting watermelon? Rolling ground beef into patties? Cutting hot dogs?

If Kris had her learner's permit, she wouldn't be here. There would've been better things to do. She'd practiced driving. Even when she was younger, nine or ten, her father would sit her on his lap and work the pedals while she steered.

She imagined what her mother would say now. That Kris was willing to risk her life for a video that only 30 people were going to watch. What a waste it would be to die to make 115 followers laugh.

When she'd asked her to call her Kris, her mom refused. Everyone else was cool with it. But Mom wouldn't, and that stung her. It was the world's smallest change. Four letters. And her mom couldn't do it.

Dad would've gotten it. He would've called her Kris without any questions. He would've been teaching her to drive in his Corvette. The thought of the car made Kris sick.

Lawn-Ba buzzed beneath her. She pictured herself falling into the blades, arms first. She couldn't get into her own head about it. She stretched her arms out. It was time. If she didn't do it now, her fantasies would get worse until they paralyzed her.

THE SUN HAD gotten higher, and the day hotter. People would be firing up the grills, drinking beers of their own. If Kris had another beer in the rest of her life, it would be too soon.

Lawn-Ba stayed underneath her. The machine was watching her the way a cat watched a bird in a cage.

She lowered herself until she was dangling above Lawn-Ba. She made sure it was still, and then she let go.

Her feet touched down on the plastic. Lawn-Ba jerked, trying to shake her off, but she managed to stay on the machine.

"Gotcha," she said.

She pressed the power button with a click. Lawn-Ba stopped moving. Its blades slowed to a stop. She smiled.

Then a voice said, "Please enter security pin."

Oh, God. What would Jed put as his security code? Probably his birthday. Her father's security pin had been his birthday. Kris had no earthly idea how she'd know when Jed was born.

She punched in 1234.

"Incorrect security pin. Please enter the security pin. You have two tries remaining."

Okay. She could do this. There must be an emergency override. He wouldn't test it without that kind of safety requirement in place, would he?

911.

"Incorrect security pin. Please enter the security pin. You have one try remaining."

No. She was so close. She put in her dad's birthday: 7/8/72.

"C'mon, c'mon," she said.

"Incorrect security pin. You are locked out."

No. Kris shook her head. This couldn't be happening. Lawn-Ba jerked forward. Kris crouched and balanced her hands on Lawn-Ba's head. There wasn't anything to grab.

"Lawn-Ba, stop!" she yelled, hoping that there would be something voice activated. The machine jerked back. It jolted forward and then stopped short. She slid but managed to stay on top of it.

This wasn't going to last, though. She looked back at the trees, waiting for Lawn-Ba to stop next to one with a low enough branch for her to climb back up.

Lawn-Ba twitched left, then right, and she crashed into the side of the house. She bounced into a window. The glass broke and cut her. She banged into the security shutter underneath. She grabbed her shoulder, pressing the glass deeper, and groaned.

"Security breach detected," the mechanical voice said.

Lawn-Ba pulled forward, and she fell off. Her back slammed off the siding. Pain shot up through her tailbone.

Lawn-Ba buzzed toward her. She rolled out of the way. If she hit the shutter again, the police would come. She raised her hand to hit it, but Lawn-Ba charged. She jumped out of the way. Lawn-Ba strafed left and right, blocking the house on either side. How did it know?

There was a tree with a low branch behind her. She backed toward it, slowly, while Lawn-Ba patrolled. She stepped on something hard, almost tripped on it. The top half of the umbrella. Carefully, she stepped over it, not taking her eyes off the machine. She patted her hand in the air in front of Lawn-Ba, as though it were an angry dog she was comforting.

She felt her back against the trunk of the tree and jumped up to grab the branch. She swung up into the tree. Lawn-Ba stayed where it was, waiting for her to come down.

KRIS SHOUTED from the tree, begging for the police. She didn't hear anything, but she hoped. She'd skipped breakfast, but she knew from Bear Grylls that she could last a couple of days without food, and at least until the next morning without water.

She imagined what it would be like if the officer who responded to her father's accident got her now. She wasn't supposed to, but she'd watched the traffic cam video of the accident. The other kids at school had been circled around a phone during gym class. A girl had screamed. A boy had gagged.

Kris had asked what they were watching.

They'd all frozen.

She'd asked again.

The girl whose phone it was, Madison, had held it out.

The video was a grainy black and white. It showed her father, in his red Corvette, heading toward a yellow light. Instead of slowing down, he'd sped up.

On the other side, an 18-wheeler was starting a slow left. Her father was trying to beat it through the intersection.

She'd heard the story twice when she'd begged her mother. The second time ended with her mother saying, "This is why you don't take risks." This was why she was trying to protect Kris.

Her father saw the light turn red and gunned it. The 18-wheeler made it halfway through the intersection. Her father slammed on the brakes. His car did a hockey stop, but it kept sliding, right under the truck. It was like something out of a *Fast and Furious* movie, but he didn't come out the other side.

It was hard to make it out exactly in the video, but something round bounced back from under the truck.

The officer who'd responded had knocked on her door hours later. Kris had been closest, and she'd opened it. He had a gray mustache and sad eyes. There was a screen door between them still, and she wished that if she didn't open it, the bad thing etched on his face would go away. It would happen to another family.

She heard a car pull up in the front drive.

"Here," she screamed. She didn't worry about who it could be or how they found her.

Lawn-Ba circled underneath her.

She'd expected police officers with drawn guns. She'd thought that this was over. Instead, her unarmed mother in an American-flag tank top turned the corner. Her mom's cell phone was in one hand, like she was following directions. Her keys were wrapped around the thumb of her other hand.

Lawn-Ba registered the new presence. It seemed to pause, to evaluate whom it had a better chance of mowing. Then, the machine charged toward her mom.

"Kristina?" her mother said. She wasn't reacting. Lawn-Ba was going to tear her mother apart. "Are you okay?"

Kris didn't think. She jumped out of the tree and grabbed the top half of the umbrella. "I'm the one you want, you stupid robot!" she yelled.

Lawn-Ba stopped, halfway between them.

"That's right. Come get me," she said. "Leave my mom alone."

"Kristina, you're bleeding. What happened?" Her mother trotted toward her. Toward Lawn-Ba. Mom had made the choice for the machine.

"Mom, no! Run!" Kris shouted.

Mothers never listen to their children, but her mother especially didn't listen. Lawn-Ba stampeded toward her.

Kris sprinted after the robot.

Her mom said, "Oh," as she processed the robot lawn mower beelining toward her.

Lawn-Ba hit Mom's foot. A spray of blood streaked the house. It arced in a circle. It sprinkled Kris' shins. Mom screamed. Her phone and her keys flew out of her hands as Lawn-Ba went farther up her leg.

Kris grabbed the umbrella and ran at the machine, hoisting the furniture debris like a pole vaulter. Another whir of blood. Mom screamed again.

She wouldn't let it kill her mom. Instead of hitting Lawn-Ba from above, she swung the umbrella like a field hockey stick.

She knocked the machine onto its back. The blade spun furiously. Blood sprinkled everywhere.

"Kristina," her mother said.

Her mom's foot wasn't cut off, but rather pared down. The toes were gone except for one, and the foot was whittled. White bone poked out. The cuts were deep. There was no way her mother could walk.

She grabbed her mom's hand. "Are you okay?"

"My foot," her mother said.

Lawn-Ba was jerking back and forth, trying to flip itself upright. Why wouldn't this fucking thing die?

She hoisted the half umbrella like it was a spear. She aimed it for the center of the blade, hoping she could break the engine. The blade caught on the umbrella. The force jerked her forward. Lawn-Ba tilted. It almost got onto its side, but she let go of the umbrella. It fell harmlessly between Lawn-Ba and the house.

If she couldn't destroy the machine, she had to get her mom out of here.

"Mom," she said.

"Goodbye, open-toed shoes," her mother mumbled.

Kris pulled her to a sitting position. "Mom, we need to get away before Lawn-Ba flips back over."

The machine was rocking back and forth, picking up momentum. It would roll over soon.

"Okay, Kristina," her mom said.

Kris got herself on the side of her mother's destroyed foot. "Stand up on your other leg."

Her mother was heavier than Kris expected. The arm across her back pushed into her cuts. The hand on the bruise sent sharp pain. Kris wasn't going to be stopped, though.

The two of them hobbled.

Kris couldn't turn back to see Lawn-Ba without throwing off her mother's arm. Instead, she attuned her ears to Lawn-Ba's blade. It was quieter going through the air, but it would be cutting grass again soon.

She spotted her mother's SUV in the driveway. They were almost there.

They reached her mother's phone. The keys were two feet ahead. "Mom, I need you to lean on the house for a second."

"I can't," her mother said.

Then, Lawn-Ba's blades started to get louder. It had flipped itself.

"We need the keys, Mom," Kris said. She let her mom go.

She grabbed the keys. Lawn-Ba was charging. Kris snagged her mother's phone and ran away from the house.

"Keep going, Mom," she yelled.

Lawn-Ba plowed toward Kris. Her mother limped toward the car farther up ahead.

Kris got ready to jump.

Lawn-Ba stopped as she left the ground this time. She was in the air, but it was still six inches ahead of her and not moving. Fool it once.

She spread her legs in the air, like she was doing a leap-frog and threw the phone down in the center.

She landed, legs wide. Lawn-Ba tore forward. It went through her legs and hit the phone. She somersaulted forward and broke into a dead sprint.

Pieces of phone flew in every direction.

Her mother was almost at the car, leaning on the house and dragging her destroyed foot. "Faster, Mom!" Kris screamed. "It's coming back!"

Lawn-Ba buzzed after Kris. She leapt out of the way. Lawn-Ba stopped. The two faced off. Lawn-Ba was stained red with her mother's blood. Kris was cut up from the table, battered from the window, and melting in the heat.

Kris stepped forward, hoping Lawn-Ba would barrel toward her.

"Come at me, Lawn-Ba," she said.

"Stay away from my daughter," her mother screamed. Mom had reached the car. She was pulling at the passenger door, but it wasn't moving.

Lawn-Ba went after Mom.

"Shit," Kris said. She fumbled with the keys, trying to hit the button. The trunk opened. The alarm blared. She chased after the machine. Finally, the locks chunked open. Her mother opened the door. Lawn-Ba was inches away. Her mother dove into the car.

Kris was three feet away, but Lawn-Ba was in between her and the door.

She leapt, like a ballerina, through the air. Her left foot hit the opening. She tried to grab onto the dry-cleaning hook. For a second, she had it, but her hand, slicked with blood and sweat, slipped.

She tipped backward toward Lawn-Ba. The machine's blades spun hungrily.

Her mother grabbed her arm. "Hang on," her mother said, and swung her into the car.

For the first time in a decade, Kris sat on her mother's lap. Mom hugged her.

Kris climbed over her mother, into the driver's seat. She adjusted her mirrors, put her hands at 10 and 2. She shifted the car into reverse. Lawn-Ba chased after it, and Kris waited until the machine was in line with the front tire.

Then she shifted into drive and jammed down on the accelerator.

Lawn-Ba died with a crunch. The blade hitting the tire was high-pitched, like the machine was screaming in its death throes. Kris didn't stop until the back tire had gone over Lawn-Ba, too.

She put the car into park and looked at her mother. "How did you know I was here?"

"Phone tracker," her mom said, applying pressure to what was left of her foot. "I'm sorry. Obviously, you can handle yourself."

"Does this mean I can get my permit now?" Kris asked.

Content Warnings

Safe at Home | *animal death*

Jailbreak | *animal death, fire, gore*

The Urge | *violence against women, extreme gore*

Social Experiment | *racial discrimination,
    violence, potential self-harm*

Hard Way | *gore*

Woman in White | *suicide, violence, gore*

Shorn on the Fourth of July | *gore*

Story Notes

No Point Crying

I temped in a mailroom of a bank's corporate office right after I finished grad school. They paid me a bananas amount of money (at least to me at that time) to make two rounds of deliveries and pickups a day. So not only did it serve as setting and inspiration for Mariano's missing-ness before he's taken, but I wrote the entire story at the desk at the end of my day.

Safe at Home

I wrote "Safe at Home" at the same bank where I wrote "No Point Crying." I've never written two stories I'm so proud of so close together before or since.

My sister inspired the voice of the narrator.

A real overpass was being demolished every night across the street from my apartment around that time. There was a crane with a jackhammer on the end, and it pulverized the

20-foot-tall support column from around midnight 'til three or four each morning. It hit with enough force that our building shook. This went on for months. When we complained, the public relations supervisor assured us that they'd put a noise-canceling blanket over the pillar. He also shared that he was suffering, too: he could hear it while he grilled.

A lot of the anger I had over that situation got into this one.

JAILBREAK

I had a blast writing a psychic battle into my novel *Say Uncle*, so when I was done, I came up with this premise for a mind-hopping psychic creature that would be the villain in my next novel. I wrote "Jailbreak" as the first story in that book, but then it petered out. I couldn't figure out where to go, and I realized that what I had was a complete story. *Tales to Terrify* published it, and the reception has been phenomenal.

Prison was on my mind at the time of writing this because my parents moved to a new house a mile away from one. From there, all I needed was Warden Carol Cardenski, my psychic warrior.

CATHOLIC GUILT

Once upon a time, I was in an MFA program living and breathing literary fiction. It hadn't been what I wanted to write (that's always been horror), but I'd had some success publishing interviews in good literary magazines.

I wrote "Catholic Guilt" on a whim after seeing the call for *Gothic Blue Book IV*, and Cina Pelayo accepted it. It was the sign I needed that I could do what I wanted (write horror) and it would be okay.

The story was inspired by a real family vacation we unintentionally took to a haunted mansion, but the family here is a grotesque parody of my family.

THE URGE

I love the story of the Vanishing Hitchhiker, but I wanted to put a new twist on it. A murderer picking her up flowed on out, and then those two opening scenes came out exactly as I pictured them. Hopefully, it felt like they ended with the bottom dropping out from under you. The rest needed more work. It's the most extreme story in the collection, a little nod to my friends at Killercon.

SOCIAL EXPERIMENT

I've long wanted to write a horrific love story. When Samantha Kolenski tweeted that she was looking for a short story to adapt into a short film, I gave it a try, which is how "Social Experiment" ended up with the tiny cast in a single location. Some of the details of my relationship with my partner are blended in with invented bits, hopefully smoothly enough that you can't tell which is which.

The other inspiration came from my psych minor. There's not much scarier than the Stanford Prison Experiment, the Milgram Experiment, Harlow's wire monkey. But honestly, we could keep going on for days about what scientists did before the dawn of institutional review boards.

HARD WAY

You may already know this because I won't shut the fuck up about it, but I trained to be a professional wrestler for six months. It was one of the coolest things I've ever done, even if I was terrible at it. "Hard Way" is a tribute to that time in my life. It's also one of the few stories I've written that I had to keep cutting because I was adding more characters, more storylines, and more things I'd learned in my time wrestling. It's something I may revisit in the near future.

WOMAN IN WHITE

I saw the film *Butterfly Kisses* and started writing this the next day. I was inspired by filmmaker Erik Kristopher Myers' concept of something moving closer and closer, but I created my own monster—the woman in white—and made it my own. There's an obvious debt to the J-horror of the '00s in the novella as well. I worried it was too indebted until I populated the world of the story with the weirdos—cousin Brian, Willow the demon mediator, and Al the metal lawyer.

The characters in this one are mostly white men, because I think that demographic of people would be most susceptible to losing their minds if they were made to face the suffering privilege insulated them from.

This, of course, leads me to my last inspiration: social media. In particular, I was thinking of calls from online activists for every person to be knowledgeable about and publicly speaking out about every single event happening in our world at all times, while our brains are designed to paint on the walls of caves. Often the causes are worthy, but no single person can (or should be asked to) fix all of them.

SHORN ON THE FOURTH OF JULY

I saw a lawn-mowing robot on a run one day, and I thought to myself, "Wouldn't it be cool if that thing went after someone?" A couple of weeks later, I had this adventure story I adore.

Acknowledgments

First of all, I'd like to thank you if you've gotten this far. I don't take it lightly that you've spent time reading my work when I know you have a thousand other options on your phone alone.

I have too many people I need to thank. I started writing these stories around 2014 and finished the last one in early 2024. Over that decade, I got a lot of help from a lot of people. So, first, to the editors who published these stories: Cina Pelayo, Max Booth III, Shannon Iwanski, and Meredith Morgenstern. It means the world to me that you took a chance on my writing. The confidence boosts those acceptances gave me was the gas that kept me going.

I started writing these stories as a graduate student at Emerson College, where I never would've been without T. Stores and Ben Grossberg, my professors and friends at the University of Hartford. The stories never would've been as good as they are without my Emerson College workshop leaders Maria Flook, Pamela Painter, Steve Yarbrough, Jerald Walker, and Kim McClarin.

The stories were written across three post-school workshops: Griffins, Nevermore Edits, and the Word Shed. Jay O'Connell, Sanjay Marwaha, Kayleigh Shoen, Zyanya Dickey, Rob Davis, Drew Tierney, Ben Biggs, Celeste, Donna Leahey, Mac Boyle, Shannon Iwanski, Amy Saker Canyon Brightley, Eris, Kaz, Johnnie Cole, Stephen Cleary, Lynne Grigsby, L.M. Brown, E.C. Fuller, Jenny Jones—and I'm sure there are a few folks I'm forgetting. I appreciate all the time you took helping me sharpen these stories!

Another gigantic thank you to all of my Patreon subscribers. Generally, people don't talk about money, but y'all are holding down my water bill every month, giving me time and energy to create not just the projects I do there, but books like this one. Whether you subscribed for a week or a lifetime, I'm honored and humbled by your support.

To my friends in the Texas Horror Crew: Grace Reynolds, Celso Hurtado, Johnny Compton, Agatha Andrews, Max Booth III, Michael Louis Dixon, Andrew Hilbert, Susan Snyder, Bob Pastorella, Leticia Urieta, Richard Z. Santos, and so many others. Your friendship and camaraderie light my fire.

I am beyond grateful to Lucas Mangum, L.P. Hernandez, and R.J. Joseph for their generous words and for the guidance they all offered beyond their blurbs.

The same gratitude goes to my mentor John Baltisberger, who walked me through all of the technical aspects of publishing a book.

Also to Matt Brandenburg, who not only beta read this book, but kept answering my questions months after.

Another debt of gratitude goes to my creative collaborators: Cass Clarke for working with me on *Horror Hangover*, and the third part of our creative hive brain, Chris Poole. You two are thousands of miles away but always treat me like part of your beautiful family. To Chuck Hewitt and Sam Edington, my Patreon beta readers and editors, who give me their time month after month. To Zac Ashford, you know what you need to do in Stamford next summer.

To Eva Mout, who absolutely crushed it on the illustrations. The book is so much better because of you!

To Sam Edington, who's been editing me into coherence since our college days.

To Zoe Tokushige, for wrestling the layout together and making this book look slick as hell.

And finally, to my family. My parents for the years they gave me to read and play with my action figures, allowing me to sharpen my imagination. My brother for carrying my uncoordinated ass through years of split-screen, multiplayer shooters. My sister for sharing my love of books and movies and giving the best recommendations through her new Instagram @offthecuffwithkb. To my daughter Sydney, for being the light in this sometimes-too-dark world. To my dog Kajal, learn to read if you want a more inspiring message; I love you. And to Betsy, the love of my life. I struggle with letting the ironic shields down sometimes. Without you, I don't know where I'd be or what I'd be doing, but I know that I wouldn't laugh half as much. I love you.

About the Author

Ryan C. Bradley (he/him) is a musician, podcaster, and the author of the novella *Saint's Blood* and the forthcoming novel *Say Uncle* from Ghoulish Books. His short fiction has appeared in *NoSleep*, *Tales to Terrify*, and *Dark Moon Digest*, among others. He co-hosts *Horror Hangover* with Cass Clarke. Learn more at ryancbradley.com.

'Ursus Art' artist Eva Mout is a Dutch illustrator and cover artist who specialises in dark art.